GAME'S END

Also by Milton Dank

THE DANGEROUS GAME

THE FRENCH AGAINST THE FRENCH

THE GLIDER GANG

GAME'S END

Milton Dank

J. B. Lippincott Company
Philadelphia and New York

Printed in the United States of America
9 8 7 6 5 4 3 2 1

U.S. Library of Congress Cataloging in Publication Data

Dank, Milton, birth date
Game's end.

SUMMARY: In this sequel to "The Dangerous Game," Charles Marceau, now a second lieutenant in the Free French Army, returns to France and its resistance movement to prepare for the impending Allied invasion.
[1. World War, 1939–1945—Underground movements—France—Fiction. 2. France—History—German occupation, 1940–1945—Fiction] I. Title.
PZ7.D228Gam [Fic] 78-12625
ISBN-0-397-31821-9

For my wife
and our daughters

". . . the sound of the trumpet,
the alarm of war."

—Jeremiah 4:19

1

The oval doorway fascinated him. Huddled on the floor of the dark cabin, Charles watched hypnotized as the varicolored lights flashed, wavered, and disappeared on the black screen of the night beyond the open hatch of the airplane. The deafening roar of the laboring engines drowned out all other sounds as the pilot slipped skillfully between the searchlights and the antiaircraft fire that probed the Normandy sky.

But it was not only the red, yellow, and orange tracers, climbing so slowly and then whipping viciously past, that made Charles shrink back against the bulkhead, nervously fingering the parachute harness that enfolded him like a cocoon. It was not only the deadly flashes of the shell bursts or the silver knife edges of the searchlight beams that made his hands tremble. It was a greater fear—stark terror of what was coming next.

In less than ten minutes, if all the violent maneuvering had not thrown the plane off course, the pilot would spot a large triangular field at the junction of two rivers. This was the drop zone. The red light would go on and Charles would have to struggle to his feet, attach the static line of the parachute to the overhead cable, stand in the open doorway, and—when the green light flashed on—hurl himself into the bullet-ripped night. It was the unknown that paralyzed him. Would he be able to stand and walk to the open hatch? Or would he cower, unable to control his fear, until the crew chief threw him out into the void? If he froze, that would be done; Peter Ivors had made this very clear at the final briefing. The mission was too important for him to refuse to jump. Under no circumstances—short of his being killed or wounded in flight—was he to be brought back to England.

Charles swallowed hard and rubbed his hands together to restore the circulation. The crew chief made his way slowly up the aisle, braced against the swaying of the plane. He paused to stare at the tense figure strapped in the parachute, then asked, "Would you like some coffee, lieutenant?"

At the younger man's nod, the sergeant produced a Thermos bottle from the pocket of his flight jacket, flicked open the top, and passed it carefully.

"How much longer?" Charles croaked.

A nearby explosion jolted the plane and the crew chief grabbed the overhead rack to steady himself. "About seven minutes," he said. "Better have a hot drink now. It's a cold night out there."

The coffee was very hot, and laced with rum. Charles sipped it eagerly and felt warmth return to his body. *Strange*, he thought, *that I should enjoy rum now.* Less than four months ago, Peter had made him drink rum to celebrate his nineteenth birthday, and he had almost choked on it.

The sergeant shoved the canister holding Charles' equipment to the edge of the doorway and stared moodily at the fireworks. "Jerry is awfully nervous tonight," he said. "Invasion fever, I guess. As if we would come over in February with snow on the ground and winter gales in the Channel."

Only half listening, Charles swallowed the last of the spiked coffee, returned the Thermos, and sank back against the bulkhead. The tension was slipping away, allowing him to concentrate on the details of his mission despite the noise and jolting. So much had happened in so short a time that the last five days were mostly a blur, but it was essential that he remember all the instructions, all the warnings, the thousand and one bits of information that had been poured into him during the briefings. Closing his eyes to shut out the frightening view through the doorway and adjusting a strap that was digging uncomfortably into his side, Charles began to put his facts into order. He started to probe his memory, beginning with the day that Peter had come to the spy school in Wales; the morning three weeks ago when he had been called off the exercise field to meet the review board. . . .

It had rained earlier and the exercise field was slippery. Under the taunting instruction of a brawny sergeant who had been a policeman in Singapore before the war, the small group of student officers had been practicing unarmed combat for over three hours. "Here now, Mr. DeJong—" the sergeant tripped the Dutch captain adroitly and placed the heel of his boot firmly on the neck of the prostrate muddy figure—"always watch the enemy's feet. Right dangerous they are. All right, Mr. Marceau. At me with the knife, please."

Charles lunged toward him, knife low and well forward. The sergeant stood flat-footed, his hands at his sides, a slight smile on his lips. At the last minute, he turned gracefully, gripped Charles' right wrist to turn aside the plunging blade, and twisted sharply. The knife flew off into space and Charles was thrown face down into the mud, his right arm numbed by a savage blow on the biceps. "Very poor showing, Mr. Marceau," the sergeant complained bitterly as he helped his aching victim to his feet. "Never come in straight like that with a knife. Slash, I told you. Use the cutting edge. That's what the bloody thing is for. Now once again, if you please, sir."

Weakly, Charles stumbled over to where the knife had fallen. When he had picked it out of the mud and turned, the sergeant was talking to one of the headquarters clerks. Clearly the news was not to his liking, for he was shaking his head in disgust.

"Colonel wants to see you, Mr. Marceau, sir. Probably saw that last horrible exhibition and wants to congratulate you on being alive. On the double now, sir!"

Charles splashed through the mud toward the ivy-covered manor house that was both schoolhouse and headquarters building. *Saved,* he thought gratefully. *Thank God for the colonel!*

They were waiting for him in one of the classrooms, four senior officers sitting behind a long table, the colonel–commandant looking bored and abstracted. Peter Ivors, handsome as ever and parade perfect in his khaki Guards uniform, was sitting in one of the front seats reading a file. *It could be an oral exam,* Charles thought, *with the professors ready to fail the candidate and one of the dons present to record the final result.* The only thing strange was the decorations on the walls: large posters of German army and police uniforms with insignia of rank; photographs of weapons, vehicles, ships, and planes; maps of Gestapo posts in the occupied countries . . . no, there had never been anything like this at Cambridge or Oxford before 1939. Or at the French university where he would be today if it weren't for the war.

Charles marched down the center aisle and stopped smartly in front of the table. Saluting the colonel–commandant, he announced, "Lieutenant Marceau reporting as ordered, sir!"

The colonel looked up surprised, as if interrupted in some private thought. He peered at the young man in the mud-stained fatigues standing stiffly at attention before him. "Ah yes, Marceau. These gentlemen—" there was a negligent wave of the hand that included the rest of the board and even managed to take in Captain Ivors—"have some questions they would like to put to you. You may stand at ease."

Relaxed but alert, Charles looked expectantly along the table. Major Simmons, the gaunt ex-Commando who taught sabotage techniques, was the first to speak. "You've been here how long now, Marceau?"

"Four months, sir, as of next Thursday." He was too old a hand to offer more information than had been requested.

"And prior to being posted here," Simmons continued, "you had completed a mission in Brittany—which is still secret—and one with the Allied forces in North Africa. Tell us about the latter, please."

They know all this, Charles thought. *They're just testing me.* "I was sent as liaison officer to the American Second Army headquartered at Bizerte. My job was to act as interpreter between the Anglo-American and French troops, with special responsibility for coordination of intelligence during the planning and execution of the landings in Sicily and later in Italy. I continued in this role until September, 1943. Shortly after the Italian surrender, I was ordered back to England. After debriefing, I was assigned here for a refresher course—"

The colonel interrupted quickly. "A refresher course. Is that what the Americans call it? You must have enjoyed serving with the Yanks, Marceau . . . being half American, that is. Tell us something about yourself, your family, and your short but spectacular career in the Resistance."

Charles cleared his throat and cast an anxious look back at Peter, but the youthful Guards captain was deep in his study of the file and to all appearances was ignoring the discussion. *I see that lurking smile, Peter Ivors,* Charles thought. He straightened his shoulders, stared at a point on the wall above the commandant's head, and began the story of his life. He kept it very short and very military:

Charles Pierre Wallis Marceau, born October 17, 1924, at St. Etienne, France. Father: Colonel Henri Marceau, presently serving in Italy with the Free French Second Armored Division. Mother: born Claire Wallis, formerly of Pittsburgh, Pennsylvania, now residing at the Solar Hotel, Cambridge. His father having been wounded fighting in Belgium in May, 1940, and his mother having gone to find him, he had been alone in Paris when the Germans had entered. Intending to flee to Cherbourg, he had changed his mind and joined a Resistance group that had formed about the ex–naval officer André-Louis Chautemps (known as Vidal) and the old Socialist René Laniel (called Kléber). The group had been decimated by arrests in November, 1941. Nine men had been shot; a boy and two women had been sent to a German concentration camp.

Charles' voice trembled momentarily as he forced himself to give this terse account of the imprisonment and death of his comrades. Major Simmons looked up sympathetically, then peered questioningly down the table at the colonel as Charles continued. "The group had been betrayed by Pascal, a British radio operator—"

"French Canadian, I believe," Captain McLeod, the taciturn radio instructor, protested mildly.

"Yes, sir. French Canadian, serving in the British army. He broke under threats by the Gestapo and gave away the whole group. I escaped over the rooftops when they came for me. Since this French Canadian was now working for the Gestapo, I had to shoot him. . . ."

Charles hesitated as the terrible night scene came flooding back into his mind. Crouching on the balcony . . . the murmur of voices inside as the Gestapo interrogated Pascal . . . the squeal of the armored shutters as he shoved them open . . . the startled look on the traitor's face . . . three loud explosions from his gun . . . Pascal, gripping his wounded shoulder, rising from his chair and stumbling blindly toward the window . . . two more explosions and the radio operator twisting and falling . . . a Nazi officer fumbling at his holster . . . the last shot and the German's face disappearing behind a scarlet mask. . . .

"Another Resistance group got me over the mountains into Spain, and after two months in a filthy Spanish internment camp, I came to England. That was the beginning of February, 1942."

The rest was routine and quickly explained. After a prolonged interrogation on the fate of the Vidal–Kléber network, he had been cleared and quickly recruited by British and Free French Intelligence. He had been given two weeks' leave before reporting to the spy school in Wales—two weeks that he had spent with his mother at a seaside resort. There was no point in talking of the instruction he had received during the arduous eight months in Wales: the long hours spent on weapons, explosives, intelligence-gathering, ciphers and codes, organization of the German police, radio sets, unarmed combat, map reading . . . the list was endless. Each of the students had been awakened in the middle of the night and dragged none too gently to the cellar by rough German-speaking men. Still half asleep, each had been pushed into a chair, blinded by a desk light, and bombarded with questions. It took a quick wit and fast thinking not to betray the cover story, the false identity with which every student had been provided in the first weeks of the course. . . . But the board knew all this even better than he.

". . . Finished the course in October, 1942. Spent ten weeks at Officer Training School. Commissioned second lieutenant in the Free French Army, seconded to British Intelligence, and left for Brittany on my first assignment in January, 1943."

Charles stopped and waited. Major Simmons leaned over and whispered something into Captain McLeod's ear; then the two of them looked expectantly at the colonel. But it was the pale, donnish Lieutenant-Colonel Alan Travers, whose specialty was blowing up things with new explosives, who asked the unexpected question.

"Who is Labru?" The tone of the voice was indifferent, but Charles sensed the tension behind the table. These were men who had made a career of searching out guilty secrets with innocent questions, and they were watching him closely, waiting for a slip.

"Labru is the bartender—was the bartender, I should say—at the Café Denis in Paris, rue Sauvage. We used his place as a 'safe house' and mail drop. He helped me . . . take care of Pascal, covered my escape after the shooting, and got me out of Paris and on my way to Spain."

"Actually," Travers insisted, "Labru was not a member of your network, but a Communist *résistant* working under the head of the French Communist party, Jacques Duclos. Was there any reason you failed to mention that?"

Charles felt the anger rising in his throat and swallowed hard. "There was no reason to mention it, sir. It is all in the records of the interrogation I underwent when I first arrived in England almost two years ago. And besides—" He hesitated as he remembered the suspicious questions of his first interrogators about his connection with the Communists in Paris.

"And besides . . . ?" the colonel asked gently.

"And besides," Charles said grimly, "Labru is my friend. He is brave and loyal and he fights the Germans. I don't give a damn what his politics are!" *There! It was said!*

The four officers behind the table relaxed and there was even a smile on Simmons' usually dour face.

"You may be interested to know, lieutenant," the colonel said, "that *that* is exactly the right answer as far as this board is concerned. 'He fights the Germans,' and to hell with his political sentiments. Admirable. But we had to be certain that you could work in harness with all sorts of people. I think we are satisfied on that point." There was a murmur of agreement around the table.

"As you have probably guessed, Marceau, you are being considered for a new field assignment. Captain Ivors will explain the details to you. I wish to make it perfectly clear that—as is customary in this service—you are free to accept or reject this mission. If you feel that for any reason you are unable to carry out this important assignment, you would be doing all of us a great favor not to take it on. There will be no questions asked about your reasons.

"Before you arrived, this board reviewed your background, training, and experience, and finds you completely qualified for the duties of this mission. Having said that, we will adjourn. Please let me know your decision." The colonel rose and left the room, followed by his three subordinates.

Charles turned and looked reproachfully at Ivors. "You told them about Labru, Peter."

"Didn't have to, Charles," Peter said cheerfully. "Very thorough lot, the school staff. They insisted on reading the transcript of the interrogation you went through when you first arrived in England. Not an unfair question, old boy. As the colonel said, you'll have to work with all sorts: Communists, Socialists, maybe even an anarchist or two."

Charles sat down next to Peter and the two young men looked at each other for a moment without speaking. Peter was tall and dark—"Cornish pirates in the family, old boy"—and his nose had been broken in a school brawl. This gave him an oddly rakish air that women found irresistible. He was twenty-one, two years older than Charles.

Almost two years had passed since they had been roommates at the spy school. At that time, they had often been mistaken for cousins. They were the same height, had full-lipped oval faces, and had dark hair, worn short, as the regulations demanded. However, Peter's eyes were brown, while Charles had the deep blue eyes of his Breton ancestors.

On graduation they had been separated, Charles going for officer training in Devonshire and Peter reporting to the War Office in London. Peter had been a lieutenant then, having received his commission earlier in a crack Guards regiment. Although they had seen each other only half a dozen times in two years, they were still close friends. In North Africa, Charles had heard rumors about several missions to occupied Europe that Peter had made and in which he had acquitted himself admirably.

"What is the mission?" Charles asked.

Peter tapped the file and grinned. "I think you will like this, Charles. It's France."

So it has come at last, Charles thought exultantly. *They are sending me back to the mainland.* In the beginning, his requests to return had been denied on the grounds that the Gestapo had distributed his picture too widely. It had been six months before the enemy had decided he was no longer in France and had removed his name from the Nazi "wanted" circulars. Only after a year had it been considered safe to send him on the mission to Brittany. And then he had been needed as liaison between the mutually suspicious French and American troops in North Africa. But he had never given up hoping for another trip to France, and now it had come.

Majo, I'm coming back. I will find you.

"What do you know about the Lilas network?" Peter asked.

Charles frowned. Officially, he should know nothing about a Resistance group in France that he had not himself worked with, but agents returning from the field often spoke too much, and when one is eager to hear all the news of one's homeland . . .

"They're operating in Normandy, I believe," he answered. "Somewhere in the Cotentin peninsula. They are chiefly responsible for what we know about the German naval installations in Cherbourg. I think they are fairly new to the game—not a large group, no radio. They send their information out through the Requin network's transmitter in Caen."

Peter nodded. "Quite correct—as of ten days ago. Right now fifteen of the group, twelve men and three women, are in a Nazi prison in Cherbourg awaiting trial. The Gestapo rounded them up at a secret meeting in an isolated farmhouse. Complete security was observed, yet when they came out of the house they found the farm surrounded by three hundred S.S. troops. Resistance was useless."

"Do you know who betrayed them?"

"No—it will be your job to find that out. We must assume that the traitor is someone in the group—or in what is left of the group—which is now in hiding. It is most unlikely that three hundred S.S. troops were just out for a stroll and decided to surround that particular farmhouse for practice. The traitor may have vanished by now, but we can't count on it."

Charles nodded sadly. Like all Resistance workers, he accepted treachery as one of the facts of clandestine life. Pascal had taught him that. Still, a traitor and French too . . . an ugly business.

"The mission," Peter continued, "is to drop into Normandy and reconstruct the network. You'll have to assemble and reinspire the survivors, and also recruit and train new members to replace the losses. And, as I said, you'll have to find and eliminate the traitor if he or she is still in the group. Unless you can do that quickly, you are bound to fail."

Charles noted that Peter was talking as if he, Charles, had already accepted the assignment. *He knows me, Peter does.*

"I understand," he said, "that there are new heavy gun sites being built all along the Channel coast, all part of the Atlantic Wall that the Germans hope will repel any invasion. Is the main objective of the new Lilas to get information on this?"

"Ordinarily, Charles, I would not discuss this with you until much later, but I can see that you want this mission, so it is only fair that you should know what you are letting yourself in for. It is a very sticky wicket indeed." Peter produced a map from the file and spread it on his lap. "Now see here. The Cotentin peninsula points at the southwest coast of England like a jolly old finger. Now here at the top is Cherbourg, the port, you know, and at the bottom, like a stopper in an inverted bottle, is the town of Carentan. Now let me ask you a question: If you wanted to prevent any troop movement into the Cotentin from the rest of France, how would you do it?"

Charles studied the map, noting the roads and railroad lines. "What sort of troops, and for how long are they to be kept out?"

"Let's say two Panzer divisions for three days."

"Then the critical points are these three bridges over the Douve River north of Carentan and the railroad bridge at St. Sauveur le Vicomte. Blowing those would prevent any crossing by the tanks or trucks of an armored division until the Germans could bring up heavy equipment and set up pontoon bridges. That would be two days at least, and maybe three or more if our planes harassed them."

Peter nodded and folded the map. "Destroying those bridges when the order is given will be the main task of Lilas. Everything else will be secondary."

Charles felt the blood pounding in his head. It was instantly clear to him. There could be only one valid reason for isolating the Cotentin peninsula in this manner: the Allied armies were going to land in Normandy and capture Cherbourg. It was the long-awaited invasion!

All through the winter of 1943, the buildup for the Allied attack on the French coast had been going on at an increasing pace. It was no secret that the opening phase of the final battle to crush Nazi Germany would be fought on the beaches of France. There was no way to hide the millions of soldiers, the thousands of tanks, trucks, and cannon, or the airfields crowded with bombers and fighters. The Germans knew that the gigantic assault that would decide the war in Europe was coming, but they did not know where or when. Without that information, they had to fortify a thousand miles of coastline, mine countless beaches, plant traps for the parachutists and gliders in the most likely fields, in the hope that they would be strong enough at the vital spot to repel the invasion.

Charles trembled as he thought of the vast armada poised in England for the cross-Channel assault on Nazi-occupied Europe. Everyone was speculating about where the landing would be—and now he knew!

His excitement must have shown, because Peter Ivors laughed and put a warning hand on his friend's shoulder. "Now don't jump the gun, Charles. Plans similar to these are being made by every Resistance group along the Atlantic coast from the Spanish border to Norway."

"What about communications? I don't want to depend on Caen. They can be broken up at any time. I'd rather have my own radio."

"You shall," Peter promised. "Use Requin until you are ready; then give us the word and we'll drop a 'piano' and a 'piano player.' Do you know anyone whom you would like in this job?"

Thinking rapidly over the available personnel at the school, Charles remembered an incident that had caused a furor in the neighborhood two weeks ago. "I want Armand," he said firmly.

"Oh God," Peter moaned. "I don't know, Charles. Right now Armand is in pretty hot water. McLeod will scream if we—"

"As a radio operator, he is tops. He has already proved this on two missions. He's an experienced parachutist. And, besides, he is tough, cunning, courageous, and full of initiative. I want him—and on a mission like this I should have everything I want."

Peter pulled a long face. "He's certainly full of initiative—imagine using plastic explosives to catch salmon. Boom! and they come floating to the surface bottoms up. Not very sporting, old boy."

"My dear Peter," Charles said stubbornly, "this is not a sporting expedition we are planning, so we can dispense with old-fashioned ideas of fair play. You British have an unfortunate habit of talking of Resistance work as a 'great game.' Very sporting, old boy, but not very realistic. So far in this 'great game,' thousands have fallen before German firing squads. Others have died horribly in Nazi jails. At this moment—" he choked and had to pause to get control of himself—"countless others are suffering hellishly in concentration camps. I admire Armand for his efficient way of fishing for salmon. Now, do I get him or not?"

Nodding unhappily, Peter made a note in his folder.

They talked quietly about the tense situation in occupied Normandy. Invasion fever was running high there, and German police controls had been tightened severely in the last month. Travel was difficult, almost impossible without permission from the Nazis, and Charles could not afford to call attention to himself by walking into the local *Kommandantur* and asking for a permit.

"We'll have to change your cover story," said Peter, "and find you an occupation that will allow you to move freely. I'll get our people working on that right away. Any ideas?"

It took Charles only a moment. "Suppose I were a Youth Leader in the French Department of Sports with special responsibility for persuading young people to go work in Germany? That nest of Nazis in Vichy that calls itself the French government has just passed a law making a period of service in Germany compulsory for all men and women from eighteen to fifty. If I have the right documents, you can be certain that the Germans will be very sympathetic to my 'mission.' All I'll have to do is avoid any real Vichy official in the area who might check on my papers."

There were a few other details to be settled; then they walked over to the colonel's office, where, standing rigidly at attention, Charles formally accepted the assignment. The colonel shook his hand and wished him luck.

That night, Charles stretched out on the bed in his spartan dormitory room and read the folder on the Lilas (Lilac) network. It was not a very thick file—the group had been operating for only six months before it was destroyed. *About par for the course,* Charles thought. *Just long enough for someone in the network to make a slip, call attention to himself—or herself—and for a traitor to be introduced into the group.*

He read the first two pages rapidly. Originally, Lilas had been part of the Requin network in Caen, but had split off when liaison had become too dangerous. The new leader had been an ex–army major, code name Titus, whose second-in-command was a doctor known as Caton. These two men had operated brilliantly, recruiting trustworthy men and women, training them for intelligence-gathering, establishing secure lines of communication with Caen by means of couriers such as railroad men. All in all, there had been about forty Resistance people in the group, and they had effectively covered the Cotentin region, even the German naval installations in the prohibited zone on the coast.

As Charles read on, he became more and more impressed. Lilas was almost a model for a new Resistance group: recruits carefully screened, excellent security, all operations monitored and data checked, no fault to be found with communications—Titus was obviously a man of considerable talent. And yet the network had been infiltrated by a traitor and destroyed in just over six months. One of the "trustworthy" men or women had been working for the Gestapo.

The thought that the traitor he would have to kill might be a woman bothered Charles, but only for a moment. He turned to the last page and continued reading.

There were really two sheets stapled together: a yellow radio flimsy with a terse report of the arrest of "about fifteen members of Lilas" at a farmhouse near Carentan on the night of January 8, 1944. The rest of the group was in hiding. An inquiry into the matter was being made by Requin. Report to follow.

The second sheet was dated five days ago and had been brought from Normandy by an R.A.F. Lysander, one of the light planes that flew into prepared landing strips at night, taking in supplies and taking out urgent mail. The text of the inquiry report was too long to be sent by radio, because of the danger that the transmission would be picked up by the German radio-location trucks that flooded the region. Still, the report did not shed much light on the cause of the disaster.

When Titus had received new orders that drastically changed the work of the network, he had decided to call in the people who would be responsible for implementing these orders. It was clearly risky to bring together so many *résistants* at one time, but the duties had to be closely coordinated and there was no way to do this without a face-to-face meeting. A farmhouse belonging to a man named Bouvier (whose son worked for Lilas) had been selected as the meeting place. It was in an isolated area twenty kilometers northeast of Carentan, on the edge of a small wood through which they would be able to escape if necessary. Summons to the meeting had been delivered by hand, only trusted couriers being used, and guards had been set on each of the three approaches to the farmhouse. Titus had reviewed the security arrangements himself and had even inspected the farmhouse and the surrounding area the day before the meeting.

On the night of Saturday, January 8, 1944, the meeting had been held as planned. The participants had arrived from different directions and at slightly different times. Nothing was known of what had taken place during the two hours that the group had spent talking in the farmhouse, because as they had left, at about midnight, they had been seized one by one on the roads and at the edge of the wood by S.S. troops. About fifteen of the group had been arrested—the exact number was still undetermined—and were being interrogated in the Gestapo jail in Cherbourg. Titus had been taken to Paris by car the next day. The inquiry was continuing with the help of Caton, who had ordered the surviving members of Lilas to scatter and hide until further notice.

Charles closed the folder and stared thoughtfully at the unpainted ceiling. That last sentence bothered him. If Caton was helping with the inquiry, he obviously had not been in the farmhouse on that fateful Saturday night. How was it that the second-in-command of Lilas had not been at such an important meeting? *Monsieur Caton*, Charles promised silently, *you and I will have a long conversation in about three weeks' time. I hope you have some very good answers to my questions.*

Three weeks was little enough time for all that had to be done. Cover story to be invented and memorized until it was part of him, like his skin; forged papers to be prepared; clothing and arms to be obtained. Getting word to the Requin network to prepare a reception committee to greet a parachuted agent; briefing Armand on the follow-up drop; waiting for Requin to send the coordinates of the field to be used; finally briefing the R.A.F., which would provide the plane. . . . Yes, three weeks was barely time enough, but he had to make the next moon period, since a full moon lessened the hazards for a parachutist. He would be able to see trees and buildings and so avoid them during the descent.

He thought about taking a quick course in parachuting, but rejected the idea almost at once. If he sprained an ankle or broke a leg during the training, he was finished as far as this mission was concerned. Besides, everyone had assured him that parachuting was more a matter of luck than of skill. You could jump a hundred times safely at the parachute school and then come down in deep water or in trees or break your legs on frozen ground on your first operational jump. Just keep your knees bent, pull up on the risers at the last minute, roll on your shoulder when you touch down, and don't let the chute drag you in a high wind. Simple enough if you do it all right the first time out. And, oh yes, pray—pray that you don't come down in front of a Nazi S.S. movie theater just as the show is letting out. That had been the end for one unlucky agent. . . .

"It's really quite easy. Just a matter of luck. Nothing you can do about that, so why worry?" Armand had said upon returning from his last drop. Charles could see him now, hunched over his cup of cocoa in the canteen, surrounded by his admiring friends—snapping black eyes, curly black hair, muscular body, strong features. And under the smiles and laughter, Armand was filled with sadness and a ferocious hatred. A Belgian Jew, he had lost his whole family in the Nazi extermination camps and burned with a lust for revenge.

There was a choking sensation in Charles' throat. As always, thinking of the fate of such a family brought the forbidden subject irresistibly to his mind.

Ravensbrück was a Nazi extermination camp.

Majo was in Ravensbrück.

If she's alive, Charles thought despairingly, *after two years and two months in that hell.*

He put the folder carefully under his pillow and turned out the light.

Three weeks until he jumped into France. Perhaps if he worked hard enough, the thought of the girl he had known as Seagull would not torture his sleep. . . .

"Lieutenant!"

It was more an order than a call. Startled from his reverie, Charles looked up at the crew chief standing over him.

"Red light, lieutenant." The sergeant moved quickly to Charles' equipment canister and fumbled with the static line.

Charles checked the light panel. The red light was dim so as not to impair their night vision, but it was definitely on. Reaching over his head, he grasped two handholds on the bulkhead and pulled himself up. Remembering Peter's last warning—"When the chute opens, it can be an awfully painful thing if a strap is loose"—he checked the tightness of the parachute straps. The static line was hooked onto the overhead cable and he jerked on it twice to make certain that it was secure. If it came loose, he would fall one thousand feet to his death. How long did it take to fall that far? About six seconds . . . then oblivion forever. *Surprising how calm I feel. Now that it's time for action, the fear is gone.*

Charles made his way carefully to the doorway and stood next to the sergeant. Looking down, he caught brief glimpses of the ground through the breaks in the low clouds that flowed by beneath the plane—light patches that would be snow, the faint outlines of fields, and once a darker irregular area that might be woods. The fireworks were gone; the antiaircraft defenses of the coast had been left behind. It all looked strangely peaceful.

The red light blinked twice, paused, and blinked again. "One minute," the sergeant shouted in Charles' ear.

Why is he yelling? Charles wondered. *I can hear him perfectly well even with this flying helmet on. . . . Of course! He's standing closer to the doorway and the sound of the engines is deafening him. Or maybe he's afraid that in my mad rush to get out I'll knock him through the hatch. And him without a chute on. . . .*

Green light!

The crew chief pushed the canister out with his foot and shrank back quickly. Pausing for only a split second to grin at the sergeant, Charles grasped the edges of the doorway and threw himself out into a howling black void.

2

Charles' only sensation was of standing in a strong wind unable to move. It came as a great surprise to him that there was none of the stomach-churning of free fall, no feeling of acceleration. His arms crossed in the approved fashion, Charles watched the horizontal stabilizer of the plane—a black scimitar blade—pass slowly over him, ever rising. The deafening roar of the engines quickly faded, and soon there was only the whistle of the wind.

Bang! The shock of the chute's opening sent a wave of pain through his chest and shoulders, but that lasted only a moment, and then he found himself floating in a vast dark emptiness, oscillating and turning slowly as the chute filled and stabilized. *Not too bad,* Charles thought. *No bones broken.*

He was drifting down through a break in the thin stratus clouds, and soon he could pick out faint details of the ground. The moon was still obscured behind a higher cloud layer, and only a weak silver light filtered through. He searched for the river that marked the western edge of his target field. It was nowhere in sight. He looked for the plane, but it was gone.

Suddenly he heard the clear metallic sound of a church bell tolling three A.M. He was gripped by the frantic thought that his parachute had been spotted and the local German garrison was being alerted, but he fought down the panic and concentrated on stopping the swinging by pulling on the shroud lines. Still, he could not drown the alarming thought that there was no church within twelve miles of his intended landing field. Could the sound of a bell carry that far? Where was the river crossing? Had there been some terrible mistake in navigation?

Trying desperately not to let his fears paralyze him, Charles stopped thinking about how close to the ground he was getting. And then, with a spine-jarring jolt that knocked the breath from his lungs, he crashed through a dense mass of weeds into icy water.

His feet held by the sticky mud at the bottom of the bog, Charles floundered about, trying to free himself from the cumbersome parachute harness. His wet gloves slipped as he struggled to twist the quick-release ring. When the straps finally fell away, he dragged himself to a snow-covered hummock and sat gasping.

The moon broke through the clouds for a moment and the silver light revealed his predicament. He was in the center of a large swamp. There was about a foot of freezing water concealed by thick weeds. This could not be the pastureland on which the reception committee was waiting for him. The canister holding his clothing, forged identification papers, and other equipment was nowhere in sight, and the white shroud of his chute was draped on top of the weeds—a dead giveaway that he was here. No farmhouse, no road, no lights were to be seen. The R.A.F. had dropped him in the wrong spot, and he had no idea where he was or how to reach the right field.

He was alone in occupied France (presumably the navigator had found the right country!), wet, muddy, shivering, and lost.

The first thing was to hide the parachute. Charles plodded back through the freezing water, bundled up the huge, sodden chute, and shoved it through a break in the ice; the mud would hold it down.

Next, he had to move on. In the brief period of moonlight, he had seen what seemed to be a wood about half a mile away. With luck, the ground would be dry there. In any case, he could not sit on the hummock like a frog. At dawn, someone would spot him and report him to the local police.

It took him almost an hour to reach the safety of the wood. The mud sucked at his boots so that every step was an effort. Grimly, he pushed his way through the weeds, shivering as the icy water found its way through the zippers of his flying suit and boots. By the time he stumbled into the trees, he was totally exhausted. But he had guessed right: under the thin snow cover, the frozen ground was dry.

There was nothing for it but to wait for first light. All his warm dry clothes, his rations, his matches, even his pistol were in the vanished canister.

Cursing the pilot, the navigator, Peter, and the school staff, Charles began hopping up and down to get his blood flowing again. It was at least an hour till dawn, and it would be a long, cold, and hungry hour.

And what would he find when the sun came up?

He came out of his hiding place behind the woodpile long enough to race down to the crossroads and read the weathered sign. Back behind the stack of rough-cut logs, he took a map from the leg pocket of the flying suit and studied it in the dim light filtering through the trees. The lettering on the sign had been almost illegible, but he had made out STE. MERE EGLISE, 8 KM. He found the town quickly enough on the map, then searched the surrounding area for two roads that intersected in a wood about five miles away. Yes, here it was—due west of the town. The intended landing field at the junction of the Merderet and Douve rivers was four and a half miles to the southeast. It might as well have been four thousand.

At first light, Charles had left his first hiding place and started walking toward the rising sun. As good a direction as any, he had thought, and, besides, one that would inevitably bring him to the Channel. He had walked about two miles, moving at a brisk pace to keep warm in the icy air, when he had spotted the road. Keeping to the edge of the woods, and ready to disappear into its depths at the first sound of a car, he had followed the road up to its junction with a second hard-surfaced road, which led off to the north. Some freshly cut logs were stacked not far from the crossroads; no doubt the woodcutters were planning to pick them up later. Before sprinting out to read the sign, Charles had waited behind this improvised cover for five minutes, listening carefully for sounds of traffic. There had been nothing, not even the chirping of birds, to disturb the ominous silence.

So now he knew where he was, but the knowledge was of little help, and no consolation. There was no point in heading for the reception field—the "welcome committee" would be long since gone. Besides, in another mile and a half he would be out of the woods, and would certainly be spotted. Better to wait until dark, then find a farmhouse and hope that the farmer was friendly.

Huddled, half frozen, behind the logs, Charles gritted his teeth to keep them from chattering. The idea of spending the entire day in the open in this bitter cold was agony, but he could not think of a better plan. Clearly, the mission was beginning badly, and was very likely to end disastrously at almost any moment.

There was very little traffic on the two roads. A German army truck carrying supplies drove past toward Ste. Mère Eglise; a farmer went by in a horse-drawn cart piled high with hay; a *gazogène*—a vehicle that burned charcoal in a cast-iron boiler strapped to its roof—puffed along noisily, running on the fumes. Then there was nothing for hours, nothing but the cold, the exhaustion, and the despair.

Charles had fallen asleep, slumped uncomfortably against the logs. He dreamed of Majo and the mission they had carried out together in Vichy. Bright sunlight, the marketplace crammed with fruit and vegetables of all kinds, the beautiful girl who had been his comrade in the underground struggle, the girl who that night had become his lover. . . .

She was speaking to him. "If you're asleep back there, wake up!"

Startled, Charles sat upright and searched the snow-covered ground between him and the woods, which was empty. But someone had spoken, and it was not Majo's voice.

"Are you there? Hurry up and answer!"

Charles peered around the edge of the woodpile, being careful to expose as little of himself as possible.

A girl in a heavy seaman's jacket, her blonde hair half hidden by a blue ski cap, was standing at the near edge of the road pretending to fix the front tire of her bicycle. She was not more than thirty feet away, working with a small wrench and looking anxiously up and down both roads.

Who was she? How had she known that he was behind the logs?

"In God's name," the girl said furiously, "answer before the Boches arrive and nab us both. I'm from Lilas. I know you're there. You left a trail of footprints out of the woods that a blind man could see. Hurry up and talk. I've been searching for you since dawn and I'm damned cold."

"I'm here," Charles said weakly, "but how did you know where to look?" He cursed himself silently for not covering his footprints.

"Never mind that now. Listen. Follow the road to Ste. Mère Eglise, but keep to the woods. About three kilometers from here, the woods end. Right at the edge is a farmhouse with green shutters and a barn in the back. You can reach the barn by cutting across an apple orchard. Get there as quickly as possible and wait."

The girl put the wrench into her tool case, wheeled her bicycle back onto the road, and pedaled off. Charles watched until she disappeared around the bend, her long hair flying like a pennant.

It took Charles over an hour to reach the farmhouse. First, two gendarmes on bicycles came down the road, and only the sound of their voices warned him in time to duck deeper into the woods. He could have sworn that they looked searchingly in his direction as they passed. Had they spotted him? He was luckier with the open staff car that came noisily over the crest of the hill. There were three German officers chatting in the back seat. One of them had the gold leaves of a general on his collar tabs. The major next to him wore the black field uniform of a

Panzer officer. Puzzled, Charles crouched behind a tree and watched the car speed down the road to the north. An armored division in the Cotentin? There had been no mention of this in the intelligence reports he had studied.

He found the farmhouse and the barn just as the girl had described them. The snow in the orchard was deep, and Charles made his way cautiously, wiping out his footprints behind him as he went. He still felt chagrined that the girl had been able to find him so easily. Of course, she'd known that he was in the vicinity and had been looking for his tracks, but still . . .

The barn was empty except for a well-fed cow who looked up from her meal just long enough to decide that he was of no interest, and then went back to contentedly munching her hay. There was a smelly blanket in the stall. Charles took off his wet flying suit and wrapped himself in the blanket, making a wry face at the strong odor. "I need this more than you, my friend," he said to the indifferent cow. "Now, if you will just tell me what I'm supposed to be waiting for. . . ."

Fifteen minutes after he arrived, Charles saw a man come out of the farmhouse, pail in hand, and limp slowly toward the barn. Tall for a Frenchman, fifty or a bit more, red-faced, with an impressive black mustache. *That's an army overcoat he's wearing*, Charles decided, *although he looks a little old for this war.*

Shutting the heavy door behind him, the farmer ignored Charles' polite "Hello," walked over to the stall, and emptied the pail of grain into the feeding trough. Without a word, he pulled a bottle from the pocket of his shabby overcoat, withdrew the cork with his teeth, and handed it over. Charles took a quick swallow and then gasped for breath as the liquor exploded in his chest and throat. Calvados! He had heard of the local apple brandy, but this was his first taste of it. After a moment he could feel the warmth flowing through his body, and gratefully he swallowed another mouthful. God, he felt almost human again.

The farmer grinned sourly. "You have to be brought up on this stuff. If you come to it too late in life, it will rot your teeth." Unable to talk with his throat on fire, Charles nodded his agreement and quickly returned the bottle. The farmer drank about a tumblerful without turning a hair, carefully put the cork back, and returned the bottle to his pocket. He examined Charles for a moment, then thrust out his hand and said simply, "Leclair."

Charles grasped the proffered hand and muttered something inane in a choked voice. Until he had a better idea of what was happening, it was a reasonable precaution not to give even his code name to a stranger. "You were a soldier?" he asked the farmer.

"Both times," Leclair said proudly. "I was at Verdun in 1916. Got a shell fragment in my leg in front of Fort Douaumont. In 1939 when war came again, I lied about my age—I was forty-seven—and made them send me back to my old regiment. There were men even older than me who had sneaked back for love of France. You should have seen us keeping up with the youngsters. How proud we were!"

The old veteran pulled a pipe from his coat, filled it with harsh black tobacco, lit it, and blew a cloud of stinking smoke toward the roof.

"Yes, we were proud to be back in the ranks because we had 1918 and our victory as memories, but the young men had nothing but defeat and fear in their bellies. In May, 1940, when the Boches attacked, we were surrounded in the Vosges Mountains. We could have held out for months, pinned down the enemy, harassed him, made him pay for every foot of our soil, but *they* had no stomach for a fight."

"Who were 'they'?" Charles asked.

"Our officers." The old farmer spat in disgust. "The divisional commander and his staff, all those who decided it was useless to die when the war was already lost. And this even before Marshal Pétain asked the Nazis for an armistice. Our general went down the hill, hat in hand, and surrendered to the first German soldier he met . . . a corporal! A whole French division surrendered to one lousy corporal! Well, not me and my buddies. No German prison camp for us. That night we smashed our rifles and made our way down through the German lines. Two of us got caught, but the rest made it home."

Shame is what drives him now, Charles thought. The shame of the defeat and the greater shame of seeing the enemy acting as master in France for the last four years. Charles remembered what Vidal had said to him the day he had joined the Resistance: "The Germans will lose the war because men and women cannot live ashamed of themselves and their country." How many had died in front of German firing squads to wipe out that shame? Vidal; that wonderful old Kléber, who—like Leclair—had been at Verdun; Raven; Mammoth . . . the list went on and on. Thousands whose names he'd never known . . . including the innocent hostages shot by the Germans for Resistance deeds they knew nothing of.

"Leclair," Charles asked gently, "what happened to Lilas?"

The old farmer grunted and puffed thoughtfully at his pipe for a moment. "Betrayed, I suppose. No other explanation for it. If you had known Titus, you'd know that he never left anything to chance. He was fanatical about security. Everything was broken up into cells. No one knew more than five or six other members of Lilas except the two top men, Titus and Caton, who knew the names and addresses of the whole group. We never used the telephone—the Nazis have listening posts on all the lines—and nothing was ever put in writing. Caton or someone in my cell always gave me orders in person at an airtight rendezvous. I reported back the same way."

"And if your security is so good," Charles said, "how is it that you're telling all this to a man you've never seen before, a man you have found hiding in your barn?"

Leclair looked solemnly at his pipe. "A messenger came by here and told me to expect a young man of about nineteen dressed in a British flying suit—" he pointed to the wet suit draped over a stall—"and that he would be wet and muddy and probably in a foul mood."

The girl, Charles remembered, *she would have passed here about an hour ago on her bicycle. Where is she now?*

"However," Leclair continued, "a British flying suit proves nothing—the Germans must have hundreds of them from the bomber crews they've shot down. So I told you something about us, enough about Lilas so you would be certain that you had a real live patriot on your hands."

"And if I was a Gestapo agent, pulled a gun, and marched you to the nearest army post? What then?"

The old farmer smiled wickedly and pointed upward with his pipe. "Then my friend in the hayloft, who has had you in the sights of his rifle for the last fifteen minutes, would have regretfully blown the back of your head off."

Charles felt the hairs on his neck bristle. In spite of the

cold, there was a film of perspiration on his forehead. Not for a moment did he doubt Leclair. Somewhere behind him, there was a rifle pointed at his head, and someone's finger was on the trigger. He did not dare turn to look. If the fellow was nervous, the gesture might be misinterpreted.

"Tell your friend to relax, Leclair," Charles said with what he hoped was nonchalance, "I'm really the man you—"

He stopped suddenly as Leclair held up his hand for silence. Someone was walking toward the barn. They could hear the sound of snow crunching, then a whistle, two long and two short trills.

"It's Caton," Leclair said. "He's arrived."

The man who came into the barn was younger than Charles had expected—about thirty, he guessed—tall, slender, with a thin bony face. He was strangely pale, and with his high cheekbones and aristocratic features he looked more like a poet than a country doctor. He was wrapped in the kind of plaid wool jacket popularly called a *canadienne*, and wore heavy work boots and a fur hat with earflaps. Clearly the good doctor thought more of comfort than of fashion. In spite of his questions about Caton's conduct, Charles felt a sympathetic attraction to him.

"Welcome to Normandy," Caton said. His voice was soft, his accent educated. "Is this your first visit?"

Charles gave him the second half of the recognition sentence quickly. "Tourists are rare in the Manche since 1939." He could see the doctor and Leclair relax, and he hoped that the man hidden in the hayloft had taken his finger off the trigger.

The doctor wasted no time on small talk. "Leclair, take Alain and watch the road." The old farmer whistled sharply and limped out of the barn. There was a rustling of hay overhead, then the sound of a trapdoor closing as Alain went out the hay-loading exit.

"We were at the field as arranged," Caton said in his quiet voice. "We heard the plane but could not see it. Two bonfires were lit. The plane seemed to have passed some ten kilometers from us. We waited as long as we dared, then dispersed. Word was passed to all our friends to watch for you. One of them spotted your canister chute and we recovered the container. We've had people out all morning searching that area for you. Louise found you first and got word to me."

Charles nodded wearily. "I was dropped on the southern edge of the Bois l'Abbé. But never mind that—I'm here now, and I think it best that we get directly to work. Is there anything new about those who were arrested since the last report?"

"Nothing. As far as we know, no one has talked, and you know how persuasive the Gestapo can be in these circumstances."

"Titus?"

"Still in Paris . . . at Gestapo headquarters on the avenue Foch. If he's still alive." There was a terrible sadness in Caton's soft voice. Whenever a network was destroyed like this, the survivors felt an overwhelming guilt. Each wondered, agonized, why he or she was spared, while friends were doomed to torture and execution. Unless that feeling was stifled in the knowledge that the struggle must go on no matter how many fell, it could turn a Resistance worker into an indecisive, frightened threat to the underground war. Charles knew this guilt well enough. Majo, Vidal, Kléber . . . he knew what it meant to lose comrades. The only remedy was action, getting back into the fight so that the sacrifices of one's friends would not be in vain—and the quicker the better.

Charles looked at Caton severely and spoke firmly. "How many of the Lilas group are still free?"

"Twenty-seven. They hid out for three weeks. Strangely enough, the Gestapo doesn't seem to be looking for them. I myself expected to be arrested at once, but nothing happened."

Charles pondered this strange turn of events. According to what Leclair had told him, every member of Lilas knew only the five or six members of his cell, plus Titus and Caton. While it was always possible that the traitor knew only the people who had been present at Bouvier's farm, he—or she—must surely know Caton, the second-in-command. But Caton had not been arrested! Was the Gestapo leaving him free to lead them to the rest of Lilas? Or was Caton the traitor? There was still the question in Charles' mind as to why the doctor had not been at the Bouvier farm.

"Have you found a new headquarters?" Charles asked.

"Oh yes. We were told to find one that would also serve for the radio. High up where the transmissions would be better. Well, there isn't much high ground in the Cotentin, you know, but we found a spot that is almost ideal. It's on a small hill about eighteen kilometers south of Cherbourg, with a clear view of the countryside in all directions. It can be approached by only one road, so it should be easily guarded. It is the Château Vaucouleurs."

"Who lives there?"

"Madame la Comtesse de Vaucouleurs and her maid."

"Are they to be trusted?"

Caton looked startled at the suspicion in Charles' voice. "Yes. I will vouch for their patriotism without hesitation."

"May I remind you, Caton, that either you or Titus once vouched for a traitor?"

The doctor's pale face was twisted with pain, and, for a moment, Charles was sorry for his cruel words. *This is a tough business*, he thought unhappily. *No place for sentiment.*

"I've had to live with that thought ever since my friends were arrested," Caton said. "Still, there can be no question about the countess. Her eldest son was killed fighting in Belgium in 1940, and her husband, her brother, and another son have been prisoners of war in Germany for almost four years. She has not been active in Lilas because of an arthritic hip, but she is with us heart and soul."

"How do I get to the chateau?"

The plan was simple enough. As a doctor, Caton had a permit—an *Ausweis*—issued by the German police that allowed him to visit patients after dark. Around nine tonight there would be an emergency call from the countess, saying that her maid had been taken ill. The doctor would fuel up his old *gazogène* Renault, drive past the barn, pick up Charles, and take him hidden in the trunk to the Château Vaucouleurs.

"What about my equipment canister?" Charles asked. It was hard to act the determined leader while wrapped in a cow blanket.

"It is already halfway to the chateau. Did you by any chance see a farmer driving a haycart through the woods when you were hiding there?" Charles nodded. "Well, your gear is under that load of hay. It will be perfectly safe. There are no roadblocks, for no one saw you come down."

"Can you get a message to London that I arrived safely and am in contact with Lilas? You might also tell them that I don't think much of R.A.F. navigation and that we'll be sending new coordinates for the field that Armand is to use. This time we'll pick one even they can find in the dark."

Caton smiled slightly at the sarcasm. "It will take four or five hours for your complaint to reach London. We're using the railroads to pass messages to Requin, and the next train won't arrive in Caen until seven tonight. But don't worry, our man on the train is completely reliable."

There was little more to say. Charles mentioned the Panzer major he had spotted. Puzzled, the doctor suggested that it must have been someone passing through, since an armored division could not have moved into the Cotentin without his knowing it.

"But his presence here must mean something," Charles insisted. "A staff meeting in this area prior to a move? In any case, add that bit of information to the message. London will be very interested. Tell them we are investigating."

Caton left shortly after this. Charles saw him stop outside and say something to Leclair and Alain. Instructions to keep an eye on him, Charles thought grimly, for the farmer nodded vigorously and looked back at the barn. Then Alain, a short stocky man with a large head, said something in a guttural voice. He was too far away for Charles to catch his words, but there was no need for that. Alain took the rifle off his shoulder and patted it affectionately.

Clearly, Caton was making certain that he did not leave the barn. *Where the hell does he think I'm going without my clothes?* Charles asked himself bitterly.

He stretched out on a pile of sweet-smelling hay in one of the stalls and began to put his thoughts in order. In the main, he was very impressed with the speed with which Caton had found him after the drop. His security seemed very good—having Alain in the hayloft was a good precaution—and the Château Vaucouleurs sounded perfect, but there was always that nagging doubt in Charles' mind. Why had Caton not been at the Bouvier farm? Why had the Gestapo not arrested him or even searched for the other members of Lilas? Who was the traitor, and what was he—or she—waiting for?

The questions began to blur in his brain. He let himself sink into the soft hay, and in a few minutes he was asleep.

3

"Our title," said the countess, "was granted to the first count, then Sieur de Montbain, by Louis the Fourteenth. I believe it was gained more by the charms and low morals of his wife than by the talent and brains of the husband—for she was a beautiful slut and he was an idiot." She smiled mischievously.

While Caton made clucking sounds of disbelief from the other side of the table, Charles smiled too. How his mother, with her American awe of the aristocracy, would have loved the Comtesse de Vaucouleurs—and how his father would have appreciated her sharp tongue!

Charles and Caton had arrived at the chateau shortly after ten. Emilie, the elderly maid, had opened the door and led them directly to the dining room. The long table was set with fine linens and crystal goblets, antique silverware, and Limoges plates. *The countess,* Charles thought, *tries to keep her traditional way of life even in these perilous times.* He felt uncomfortable sitting in the midst of such elegance in a wet, mud-flecked flying suit.

Leaning heavily on a cane, the countess made a grand entrance through the ornately carved doors that led to the salon. Although there was no flourish of trumpets, no uniformed majordomo, the visitors were intensely aware that Madame Agnes Lucille Marie Toussaint de Montbain, Comtesse de Vaucouleurs, had arrived.

Sitting at the head of the table, turning politely to talk to each of her dinner partners in turn, she reminded Charles of a great lady of the past. *She must have been gorgeous as a girl*, he thought. Even now, beauty showed in that lovely skin, those fine aristocratic cheekbones, that sensitive chin. Her voice was a touch husky from age, but there was a note of command in it that left no doubt as to who was the chatelaine, the mistress of the chateau.

She talked to put them at their ease, as if she were entertaining two visitors passing through her domain on the king's business, rather than two hunted men, two "terrorists" wanted by both Vichy and the Germans. She told stories of her family in the Great Revolution, in the African campaigns, fighting the "Prussians" in 1870 and 1914. She spoke proudly of her dead son, Etienne, who had fallen before the first savage thrust of the German attack. The captivity of her husband—"who is really too old for the army, but he dyed his hair and lied about his age"—and of her younger son she discussed without tears. The family had been sending men off to the wars for centuries. The women had had hundreds of years to learn how to accept the capture and death of husbands, sons, fathers, and brothers. It was an old story, too often repeated, for the de Vaucouleurs.

"You will have Etienne's room," she said to Charles. "I think he would be happy to know that his room is being used by someone who comes from England to fight the enemy. Have no fear—the Germans seldom come here.

Once long ago, they tried to requisition my home for some awful antiaircraft unit, but I blistered the ears of their commander in Cherbourg, and now they leave me alone. I assume you will have your own people watching the road?"

The doctor nodded. "With your permission, of course, madame."

"With or without it, I suspect," the countess said, and laughed. "You must learn to be less polite, Caton. After all, this is war."

Nibbling at his dainty portion of chicken and potatoes and sipping his wine, Charles made a mental note to talk to Caton about extra supplies of food for the chateau. Although everything was deliciously prepared—Emilie was a marvelous cook—there was precious little of it. With the German army quartered nearby, food was in short supply. Charles knew his presence would put a strain on the provisions; then, too, Armand would arrive soon, and his would be another mouth to feed. Lilas would have to put a little subtle pressure on the neighboring farms to hold back some of the food from the enemy garrison to supply the chateau.

By the time Armand appeared twenty-four hours later, Charles had set the wheels in motion and was ready for action. At least part of Lilas was back in the struggle.

Charles had personally selected the field in which the radio operator would land. Caton had vetoed his first choice as being too close to Leclair's farm. "No point in having the Germans nosing about there if the parachute is spotted."

This time a wooden T soaked in kerosene was lighted as soon as the plane was heard. Charles felt it was worth the risk; when they turned the T into the wind, the pilot could judge which way the chutes would drift and plan his approach accordingly. Two minutes after the fiery cross started to blaze, the "welcoming committee"—Charles, Caton, Leclair, and Alain—saw two parachutes float down at the far end of the field. They doused the fire and ran toward the "piano player" and his "piano."

When they reached the spot, Armand was crouched behind his bulky radio canister, covering the approaching figures with a pistol. Charles shouted the recognition sentence and received the correct reply.

Huddled on the floor of the back seat of the Renault, Armand bubbled with joy at being back in France and at the prospect of action. It took all of Charles' tact to keep the radio operator's exuberance under control. Once, Caton rapped urgently on the steering wheel—the danger signal!—and they held their breath as a long convoy of trucks roared past. Luckily, the enemy patrols were not searching the roads that night, and they arrived safely at the chateau at three in the morning. The countess, exhausted by a long night's vigil, was asleep in an armchair in the library.

Charles had prepared the attic for the radio by partitioning off a small area at the very back and drilling a tiny hole through the roof for the copper wire antenna. He took Armand up to see it before they had been in the chateau ten minutes. Armand grumbled at the cramped quarters and the tiny entrance—"I'm not a midget, you know"—but Charles pointed out that by piling old furniture and boxes against the separating wall, they could make the radio secure from any but the most thorough search. Also, after Armand crawled through the narrow "rathole," he could move a box to close off the entrance and be completely hidden. The transmitter, which had been stowed in the trunk of the car, was carried to the attic and quickly set up.

According to the schedule that Armand had been given before his departure, the first contact with London was to be attempted at five A.M. by sending the identification signal WSR for ten minutes. If no answer was received, the radio was to be shut down until four P.M., which would give Armand time to check the transmitter and make certain that it had suffered no damage in the parachute drop.

As he slid the wire antenna through the hole in the roof, Charles remembered the first time he had assisted at a clandestine radio transmission. Was it really almost two and a half years ago that he, Vidal, and Kléber had waited anxiously in a shabby back bedroom over a Montmartre garage while Pascal—not yet a traitor—hunched over his key, trying frantically to reach London before the Nazi radio-location truck found them? One of the first messages they had received had sent Charles to Vichy to pass important orders to the redoubtable Max, chief of the Resistance in the south of France. Now Max was dead, tortured to death by the Lyons Gestapo; Vidal and the others had been shot; and Majo, who had accompanied Charles on that trip to Vichy, was suffering the horrors of the Ravensbrück death camp. . . .

There was a short delay when they found that the wiring in the chateau was so old that the electrical outlets in the attic would not fit the radio plug. Armand quickly unscrewed the outlet plate, cut off the plug, and made direct contact to the mains. It took only a few minutes to insert the correct crystal for the frequency London would listen to at five o'clock, warm up the set, and send out the first code query: "WSR, WSR, WSR." Then Armand switched to the receiver and listened. No reply. Again the radio operator tapped urgently on the key, then pressed the earphones tightly against his ears, as if he could squeeze an answer out of London by sheer pressure. No reply.

With Caton timing the transmissions (they could not risk being on the air more than ten minutes, because in fifteen the enemy would have a good fix on their position), Armand continued to call the English station. "Are they all out to tea?" he muttered savagely when the earphones stayed dead.

Finally, after six attempts, the sputtering sound of the awaited answer came through the headset: "WTI, WTI, WTI CALLING WSR. GO AHEAD." London was listening. They were in contact with their friends.

Although Lilas' first message was short, so much time had been spent in establishing contact that Charles scratched out the first six message groups. They had concerned Armand's safe arrival, which would be obvious from the fact that the radio was in operation. Armand transmitted only a request for the dispatch of explosives to be used to blow the bridges. Charles desperately wanted to know London's reaction to the news that there was a Panzer officer in the Cotentin, but did not dare risk staying on the air long enough to hear it.

Armand closed the power switch and pulled the antenna down into the attic. "Now what?" he asked jokingly.

"Two things," Charles said quietly. "First, we start rebuilding the network. That means getting in touch with the surviving members, recruiting new *résistants,* training, assigning tasks for the sabotage missions, tightening security—" he glanced at Caton, who did not react—"and reconnoitering the bridges we will attack."

"And second?" Caton asked.

Charles looked him full in the face for a moment before answering. "Second—and it must be done quickly—we will find the traitor and kill him!"

Armand wrapped the long copper wire into a coil and placed it carefully in the radio case. "Believe me, Caton," he said with a grin, "I'm more frightened of this guy here than you are. I can't help remembering that the last traitor he killed was also a radio operator."

Caton smiled feebly, but Charles did not even hear the joke. Pretending to study an old portrait in the corner of the attic, he was planning his next move. He decided to start by talking to Louise.

"Kellerman is an Alsatian name," the girl said. She picked a dead leaf from an oak tree and looked at it carefully. Charles could see that she was embarrassed to be talking about herself to a stranger, so he kept his eyes fixed on the garden ahead. They were walking in the park behind the chateau among the bare trees and flower beds. The gravel path was striped by the wintry sunlight filtering between the leafless branches.

"My family has lived in Alsace for centuries and we have always been French, even under the Germans. My father was professor of European history at the University of Strasbourg. When the Boches arrived in 1940 and annexed the province, he moved us all to Lyons. Almost the whole faculty came with us. We called it showing our patriotism with our feet. My father wanted me to go on with my studies, but it was impossible to concentrate on literature with the Germans occupying our country, so my brother and I joined a Resistance group—it wasn't hard to find. We printed pamphlets and collected information, military intelligence really."

They turned on a side path that would take them past

the pond, and, as they did, Charles stole a glance at her. Under the pea jacket she was wearing a white blouse and red skirt that suited her perfectly. Her long blonde hair flowed down her back and her deep blue eyes were fixed on the horizon. A small nose slightly uptilted . . . she was biting her lower lip as she concentrated on her story. With a guilty start, Charles remembered that Majo had the same habit. And yet Louise was not in the least like the girl he had lost—taller, for one thing, fair where Majo was dark—no, there was little resemblance.

"Like most Alsatians, I speak fluent German, so I was very useful in the work. I got a job as a typist in the local German army purchasing bureau and kept my ears open. Oh, we sent a lot of interesting news to London. We lasted three years, which must be pretty near a record, because we were real amateurs, but in the end we were betrayed. My brother and I got out at the last minute before the Gestapo arrived at our house. Another network smuggled us out of town and onto a train to Normandy. That was almost a year ago. My brother was soon on a fishing boat for England. They wanted me to go too, said it was too dangerous for me to stay in France, but I would not leave."

The soft voice held a note of bitterness now. "My father was shot as a hostage two months after we fled. My mother was sent to a concentration camp in Germany—I don't know which one. So my brother is in the Free French Army, and I am here."

He knew better than to offer sympathy. The girl was proud, and, besides, she knew that hers was not an uncommon story. Her father, his comrades in Paris—the list was long, and got longer every day. Her mother, Majo . . . and tens of thousands of others.

They reached the pond and stood looking down into the

still depths. It was surprisingly warm this afternoon. The sun was bright and the traces of snow had disappeared from the park. A lovely time to walk with an attractive girl, and Charles was all too conscious of the fact that he found Louise Kellerman very attractive. But he forced himself to concentrate on the problem at hand.

"Mademoiselle," he said hesitatingly, "do you have any idea, any suspicion, who might have betrayed Lilas?"

She stared into the water and shook her head. "In Lyons, the traitor was a woman who had fallen in love with a German soldier. She did it to please her lover and to make herself important in his eyes. But here . . . no, I have no idea. Remember, I know only Titus, Caton, Leclair, Alain, and one or two others. Security was very tight. My main job was as a courier, carrying messages down to the train for Caen and picking others up the next day. One thing I am certain of—you can trust Caton."

I can trust no one, Charles thought miserably. Not the good doctor who should have been at the Bouvier farm; not even a lovely young girl, born in a province that had been German for fifty years, who spoke fluent German, and whose flight from Lyons might have been arranged by the Gestapo. *No one can be trusted; everyone has to be checked.*

They walked back slowly, talking about books and writers. They discovered that they both adored Balzac, François Villon, and Flaubert, but Louise argued that *Madame Bovary* was overrated.

It took three days for London to check its network in Lyons. Louise Kellerman's story was verified in all details. Her brother was now serving as a bomber pilot in North Africa. Clearance was given to employ her in any position of trust.

Armand grinned wickedly at Charles' deep sigh of relief. *He knows that I spoke to Louise first for personal, not tactical, reasons*, Charles thought.

For the next two weeks, Charles traveled widely through the Cotentin, meeting with the demoralized survivors of Lilas. Everywhere he found fear, discouragement, and anxiety over the fate of arrested comrades. New to the clandestine war, those still at liberty had found it hard to absorb the first cruel blow—"to feel the pain and still go on," as Charles put it to Armand. Caton was apparently so crushed by the tragedy that he was unable to inspire his people—or was he trying to keep them out of the fight? It was Charles, meeting singly or in small groups with frightened *résistants*, who eventually was able to put steel in them again.

He wasted no time on sympathy or pity. "No one can stop you from feeling anguish over losing friends—especially to the Gestapo. We all know what they must be going through even now. But if you quit, if you leave the fight against the enemy, then their suffering will be in vain. What you must do is hard, but you must do it. Your friends are gone. Forget them. Put them out of your minds until this filthy war is over. Otherwise you will never be able to carry on. You will lack the firm resolve, the cunning that will keep you alive. Your fears will make you apprehensive, nervous instead of wary; you will make mistakes in security. You'll find yourself failing to make a perfectly safe rendezvous because a stranger on the street looks at you queerly and your feverish mind turns him into a Gestapo agent. Believe me, I know what I'm talking about. I've lost friends, dear friends, to German firing squads. The only thing that makes any sense now is to make certain that their sacrifice was not in vain."

Charles succeeded with most of the Lilas survivors because the patriotism that had taken them into the Resistance in the first place was still there, but twice he failed. A grocer named Didot, whose brother had been taken at Bouvier's farm, asked to be excused. "My mother is old," he told Charles, "and this has been a bitter blow for her. If I am arrested too . . ." He left the rest unsaid, but Charles knew what he was thinking. Shaking Didot's hand, he thanked him for his past services and promised that he would not be disturbed again.

The widow Seurret was a different case: her nerves were shot. Weeping, wringing her hands, she begged Charles to understand that she could not return to the struggle. "I've always been very delicate," she protested, "and this strain has been too much. Every minute of every hour, I wait for the Gestapo to come and drag me off to their awful cellars. No, I can't do it. I'd only be a danger to you all."

Charles felt a deep pity for the haggard woman. *She's as much a casualty of this war,* he thought, *as any soldier who breaks under a prolonged bombardment.* He held her hand and comforted her, saying that they were all proud of her, that they would remember her past work for the cause. When he left her, she was sitting at her kitchen table, crying softly.

In the end, twenty-five of the survivors were back in action. Charles estimated that the sabotage missions would require at least fifty. Recruiting twenty-five new members would not be easy.

One night, alone with Armand in the attic just before a transmission period, an exhausted Charles unburdened himself. He told the attentive radio operator what it had cost him to be so hard with the poor frightened *résistants.*

"At times I could barely keep from choking as I told them to forget their friends, to wipe them from their memories, to think only of the fight for France. What right have I to force them to risk their lives again?"

Armand was silent until the anguished tirade came to an end. Then the radio operator was ready with his answer. "Listen, my friend, we have had the bad fortune to be born at a miserable time for our countries. We didn't ask for this struggle; it was forced on us, and we have paid a terrible price so far. I lost my whole family, and you, your comrades. If we stop to worry about everything we have to do to continue to fight, we won't have any strength left for the enemy. This self-doubt you indulge in is bad, both for you and for the people you have to lead. Stop thinking about it, and let's get on with the job we have to do. Only the mission counts."

"I've told myself all that," Charles said. "I've tried to make myself cling to the thought that the lives of thousands of men may depend on how well we do our duty here and now. We have to free our two countries from Nazi tyranny, have to try to save the lives of all those who might still fall before German firing squads and avenge those who have already fallen. Don't you think I know all this?" His voice broke as strong emotion gripped him. "But it's damned hard to risk the lives of others."

Armand shrugged his shoulders. "I'm glad that I only take orders, Charles, and do not give them. Commanding others in work like this is a lonely and agonizing job. It is inevitable that some of the group will be lost. All our experience tells us this will happen, but do we quit? Do we crawl into a safe hole and hide until it is all over? No, we do our task as best we can. The others know the risks, and they know that we share the danger with them. You are not asking anyone to do anything you would not willingly do yourself. Certainly you would prefer to carry on the work alone if you could. But you can't. You need Lilas to accomplish the mission. *The mission,* Charles. You must think only of what we have to do. If people fall in the fight—well, they fall. We are all soldiers here."

There was a short silence; then Armand continued, "Harden yourself. You've been in this struggle long enough to know that there can be no room for sentiment. We have a tough job to do. Let's do it."

So, Charles thought, *the "great game" does not allow time out for brooding over injuries. . . . But Armand is right. The mission is everything.*

He resigned himself to the task at hand. There was still a traitor somewhere in Lilas, and he or she must be found very soon.

At night, locked in his room, he struggled with the puzzle, examining it from all angles. Gradually, from his talks with the remaining *résistants,* he narrowed the list of suspects to three men: Caton; a young truck driver named Decius; and the stationmaster, Frontin. All three should have been at Bouvier's farm, yet none had been there when the arrests were made. Titus must have summoned his second-in-command, the man in charge of transport (Decius), and the man who knew most about the railroad lines that the Germans used to bring equipment and reinforcements into the Cotentin (Frontin).

Charles went over the logic of his argument again and again. It would be ghastly if he made a mistake. First, Titus was incredibly strict about security. Thus, no one who had not been ordered to the rendezvous should have known of it, and no one who had not been invited could have betrayed it. Of course, it was possible the traitor had been at the meeting and was now many miles away, hidden by the Gestapo. But it seemed more likely that the Germans had sent him back to ferret out the rest of the Lilas network. Especially if he had an airtight excuse for not being at the rendezvous.

Three men—and one of them almost certainly a deadly traitor. But which one?

Each man had a story to tell. Caton had been ready to leave for Bouvier's farm when he had received a telephone call: a woman was desperately ill, perhaps dying, in a village some thirty-two kilometers away. . . .

The caller pleaded with the doctor to come immediately. Torn between his professional duty and his obligation to the Resistance, Caton sent a message to Titus that he would be late (the messenger was among those arrested at Bouvier's farm). When he arrived at the address given him, Caton found an elderly woman stricken by typhoid fever and an anguished husband fluttering about wringing his hands. It took the doctor most of the night to bring the woman back from the edge of the grave. Twice her vital signs disappeared, and twice he managed to snatch her from death. At dawn, she was sleeping fitfully; the fever was down and there was some color in her cheeks. He returned to his office for more vaccine, and there learned of the arrests at Bouvier's farm. . . .

All this Caton told to Charles in the most professional manner, as if he were reading from a medical chart, but there was a dullness in his voice and a sadness in his eyes that belied his calm tone. It was clear to the younger man that Caton still felt guilty at not having shared the fate of his friends.

The story checked out in every detail: the husband swore that the doctor had saved his wife's life that night and had not left the house before dawn. With a deep sense of relief, for he liked Caton, Charles turned to the other two names on his list.

Decius was interviewed at the garage where he worked. He told Charles that he had received word to be at the rendezvous, but claimed that his truck had broken down on an isolated road, that he had been too far from Bouvier's farm to walk. "I spent most of the night working on that damn carburetor," the burly truck driver said, "and didn't get back here until nine the next morning. No, no one saw me on the road; it's not often used, which is why I chose it to get to Bouvier's. Anyway, I was lucky that no Boche patrol spotted me. It would have been hard to explain what I was doing out so late." All this was offered in a belligerent tone of voice, as if Decius suspected that he would not be believed.

There was a big question mark next to Decius' name on the list Charles kept in his head. A story that could not be checked was suspicious indeed.

The stationmaster, a red-faced, sullen type, denied having received any orders to be at the rendezvous. It was Titus who ordinarily gave him his instructions. "Maybe he had a lot on his mind and forgot to tell me," Frontin said. Titus was now in a Gestapo jail in Paris, so this could not be checked. "But in any case, I was stunned to learn of the arrests. Don't think it was easy for me, either. I couldn't duck into hiding, like the others." *Why does he say that so proudly?* Charles wondered. "After all, I'm the stationmaster. If *I* had disappeared the day after the raid, the Germans would have known instantly that I was involved."

There was another question mark, next to Frontin's name.

The night after he talked to Frontin, Charles spent several hours thinking about the explanations and weighing the probabilities. Caton was guilty of putting his professional duty first, but no one could blame him for that. It was his profession to save lives, not to plan sabotage. The truck driver had no alibi and could have conveniently damaged his own truck so as not to be able to make it to the rendezvous. And the stationmaster, Charles was convinced, was lying. From everything that had been said to him, Charles was quite sure that Titus could not have failed to include the railroad man in a meeting at which the *résistants* would plan to blow up the tracks used by the Germans to supply the Cotentin. Surely the stationmaster would be in the best position to know which tracks these were. And how could Titus, that paragon among Resistance leaders, have forgotten to give so vital an order? No, there was something suspect about the stationmaster's agitated denials. Still, suspicion was not proof.

"Shoot them both," Armand suggested bitterly when the problem was presented to him. Caton started with horror and his protest was vehement, but Charles simply smiled at a poor joke.

"I can't kill a man for a faulty carburetor or for failing to receive orders," Charles said. "It is highly unlikely that Decius and Frontin are both traitors—possible, but not probable—and, besides, what would the others think if we shot an innocent man to make certain of getting a guilty one? Not too good for morale, eh?"

Then he quietly explained his plan.

"I don't understand," Frontin said nervously. He kept throwing anxious glances down the street toward the town square, as if he were afraid that they would be detected.

Charles shrugged his shoulders as if it were not important and even managed a laugh. "It's very simple. The Germans send trainloads of ammunition through here to the coastal guns near Cherbourg. They have to tell you the makeup of the train and the time it will be passing various points on the line so that you can clear the tracks for them. All you have to do is get word to us in advance when the next train will be passing over the bridge on the Merderet at Voison. Just leave your signal lantern on the bench in front of the station and one of us will contact you for the information."

The stationmaster was sweating now. "The Boches will know that you were tipped off, and they'll come right to me."

Charles shook his head. "Come now, Frontin, we're not stupid. The bridge is old and it has been a hard winter. If one of the ties is loose because of the frost and thaw, and if a rail should therefore be slightly out of alignment—well, who could prove it was not an accident?"

"You don't know the Gestapo. They don't trust anyone. They'll be swarming all over this place in an hour, dragging people out of their homes and giving them the third degree. Someone will talk, and then it will be my neck in the noose."

"No one will talk," Charles said.

From the window of Leclair's farmhouse, Charles could see two dim figures digging at the edge of the woods. It was late and the light was failing fast. There was a chill in the air, not unusual for early March in this part of the country, but the shiver that ran through Charles' body had nothing to do with the temperature. He was feeling revulsion for the work he had to do—the same disgust he had known after killing Pascal and the German S.S. officer. *What a filthy war!*

He turned from the window, adjusting the air-raid blackout curtain carefully, then walked to the table and lit the single candle. The kitchen was small, and the flickering yellow flame threw an ominous shadow on the wall. *What a place for an execution,* he thought miserably. Sitting in a rickety chair, he stared at the door through which the traitor would soon walk for the last time.

It had all been carefully planned. Caton would meet the man on his way home from work. As they walked along chatting, two men would approach them, flash German police cards, and ask for their papers. There would be some question about the good doctor's card, and the two of them would be escorted to a car (a black Citroën such as the Gestapo favored) and told they would be driven to "headquarters" for verification of their papers. The other man would not be worried. After all, it would be the doctor who was under suspicion, and at Gestapo headquarters there would be someone who knew the German agent and valued his services.

As they left the town, Caton would put a pistol to the man's ribs. Then he would know and begin to tremble.

In the gathering gloom at the edge of the woods, a grave was being dug. The Resistance had no jails in which to keep prisoners until after the war.

A car turned off the road into the gravel path that led to the farmhouse. Charles listened to the sounds as it approached: the clatter of pebbles against its underbody, the squeal of the tires as it stopped, then a mumble of voices and the slamming of car doors. He was here, the traitor who had sent his comrades in Lilas to the Gestapo torture cells. A Frenchman who had betrayed his fellow countrymen.

Someone stumbled outside the door and there was a stifled curse. Then the door opened and a pale Caton entered, followed by two men dragging the panic-stricken Frontin.

They flung him into the chair opposite Charles, then moved back into the shadows and waited. There was a long silence as they stared at the huddled figure, his face sweat-stained, his eyes red with tears, his whole body racked by sobs.

Trembling, he raised his head and stared pleadingly at his accusers. "I'm innocent," he said in a choked voice. "I swear that. . . ."

Charles tried to find hate in his heart, but there was only an overwhelming grief at what had to be done. He cut off the anguished plea with a sharp downward motion of his hand. "All that is useless, Frontin. We know that you betrayed Lilas *and* our plan to attack the ammunition train. Early this evening, a company of German soldiers moved into the woods overlooking the bridge across the Merderet at Voison. They're still there, waiting for the saboteurs to loosen the tracks. Also, the Germans have substituted an armored train for the usual freight wagons and are sending a small engine ahead of it to find the dislocated track. This we know: only *you* could have told them where the attack would take place, because we never really intended to tumble that train into the river. I spoke of doing so with no one but you—and I didn't tell the enemy. So you see, it is useless to protest your innocence."

The terror-stricken Frontin moaned and buried his head in his hands. Behind him in the darkness there was a movement forward, and the two men gripped his shoulders. Charles waved them back.

"Nothing can save you, Frontin," Charles said softly.

"You know what we have to do. But you are a Frenchman, and we are going to ask you to remember that and to do one last service for your country. Yes, the country you betrayed . . . and the comrades who are suffering for your betrayal."

The traitor looked up hopefully and stared almost eagerly across the table. Charles shook his head.

"No, Frontin. There is no salvation for you in this—only peace for your soul in knowing that you have undone a small part of the damage you did to our struggle. Will you help us now, knowing it will change nothing for you, but may be all-important for us?"

This was the part that Charles hated most, but he had to have the information that Frontin possessed. If necessary, he would lie and promise Frontin his life in exchange for it. But that lie stuck in his throat, and, besides, he did not think the traitor was fool enough to believe it. Frontin knew that he would never be permitted to leave the farm alive. His very existence was a deadly threat to all of Lilas. No, there could be no forgiving, but perhaps there was a spark of patriotism or decency left in the man. Who could know what had led him to this betrayal?

There was no sign from Frontin, just a fixed stare. *His eyes are dead already,* Charles thought.

"Who was your contact with the Gestapo? We know that you have never been to their headquarters and have never written to them. How did you pass on your information and receive your orders?"

The huddled figure seemed not to have heard. Charles put his hand lightly on Frontin's shoulder and felt the shudder that ran through his body. "Play the man and I promise you that there will be no pain," Charles said softly.

Then the words came with a rush, the whole terrible

tale of betrayal: how he had been summoned to the rendezvous at Bouvier's farm . . . had made the "innocent" telephone call to an insurance bureau in Cherbourg . . . had delivered the coded message while talking of premiums and lapse dates . . . had left the farmhouse first and had been allowed to pass through the S.S. lines. It all came out in an eager breathless voice, as if the man were confessing in the safety of a church.

Frontin had sold Lilas to get his son released from a German prisoner-of-war camp. What he had not known until too late was that his son had died of typhus two years before. The Gestapo had kept him hoping all this time—hoping and betraying. After the arrests at Bouvier's farm, they had told him of his son's death and had laughed at his anguish. Then they had threatened to expose him to the Resistance unless he helped them locate the rest of the Lilas network.

"Why wasn't Caton arrested?" Charles asked. "You knew him, and at the meeting you must have learned the names of others. Why didn't you point them out to your Gestapo friends?"

Frontin shook his head without looking up. "After they told me about Bernard . . . my son . . . after they laughed at me . . . Besides, I could not denounce Caton. By then I knew why he had not been at the farmhouse. . . ."

"Well?"

"The woman he saved that night is my sister."

Charles stared at the pitiful figure of the traitor. For love of his son, he had betrayed his country and his comrades; for love of his sister, he had saved Caton from the Gestapo. From shame at being a dupe, he had refused to denounce anyone else. How could one understand such a man?

Frontin was still babbling, repeating his confession again and again, as if there could be mercy in the constant repetition. Or perhaps he thought that as long as he was talking, they would not—

Charles got up from the chair and walked out of the kitchen. There was no need to give any orders. Everyone knew what had to be done.

He strode down the gravel path toward the car thinking about some troublesome details of the sabotage plan. At least it occupied his mind. He did not want to think about his own part in what was happening in the farmhouse. He had promised the traitor that there would be no pain, and he depended on Caton to see that the two men Frontin had taken for Gestapo agents kept his word.

Louise was standing by her bicycle next to the car. "What are you doing here?" he said furiously.

She did not seem upset by his anger. No doubt she knew about Frontin. In any case, she had only to look over to where the grave was being dug. The girl was no fool.

Louise took an envelope from one of the pockets of her pea jacket and handed it to him. "Armand said it was urgent."

He grunted, tore open the envelope, and read the decoded message. Then he took out his lighter, burned the radiogram and the envelope, and ground the ashes under his heel.

There was a muffled cry from the farmhouse—not loud, but it made Charles shudder. Louise watched him for a moment, then asked, "Was it important?"

"What? Oh, the message—no, not terribly. It's a reprimand. London is becoming impatient about our failure to find the traitor."

* * *

In the weeks that followed, Charles threw himself almost desperately into preparing for the sabotage of the bridges. By filling his hours with making plans, training the new recruits, reconnoitering the terrain in the vicinity of the targets, and a thousand and one other tasks, he tried to forget Frontin.

The execution of the traitor was reported to London in a terse message that hinted at Charles' chagrin at the undeserved reprimand. When London radioed its congratulations, Charles refused to acknowledge the praise. He had done what had to be done, but he was not proud of it. "I wish London would use less air time for this nonsense," Charles said when Armand showed him the congratulatory message. "Don't answer that, but ask them about the high explosives they promised. Unless, of course, they expect us to blow down the bridges by huffing and puffing on them."

More and more, Charles found himself working long hours with Caton, Armand, and Louise as his staff. Caton had found a new vigor and initiative. Charles guessed that the doctor's earlier lethargy and confusion had come from a fear that he, Caton, would have to take a human life if he uncovered the traitor. Now that that problem had been handled by Charles, Caton was showing himself to be a superior second-in-command.

Armand handled the radio traffic and worked with Charles on the technical side of the plan to destroy the bridges. He still grumbled occasionally about his "rathole" and the tiny radio room, but Charles knew that this was the Belgian's way of relieving the tensions of his long confinement in the chateau.

Louise was their courier and their contact with the other members of Lilas. It was Louise who brought back from town the news that the Gestapo had been making inquiries about the vanished stationmaster. There had been the usual threats when no one came forward with any information as to Frontin's whereabouts, but nothing was done to harm the townspeople.

At first Charles had tried to think of Louise Kellerman simply as a valuable member of the group, a highly competent courier, tireless, discreet, and security-conscious, but he soon found that he enjoyed having her near, and that he worried about her safety when she left the chateau. This worry, disguised as concern for the success of her mission, did not escape his two right-hand men. Caton only smiled knowingly, but Armand began to sigh longingly like a disappointed lover and to quote poetry about "love, sweet love that rises in the Spring." Furious, Charles demanded that he stop the jokes, but the radio operator swore that he himself was burning with unrequited love for Emilie, the countess's maid.

Grumbling, Charles denied that he was attracted to Louise. To himself, he said that the idea was unthinkable. Majo stood between him and any other woman. Still, he found that when he was making out the list of the four sabotage groups that would attack the bridges, he automatically put Louise's name, with his own and Armand's, in the group that would handle the bridge at St. Sauveur le Vicomte. "I may need a courier," he told the grinning Armand.

In the middle of April, the long-awaited high explosives began to arrive. Reception committees were organized to gather up the canisters and hide them in barns and cellars until Decius could collect them in his truck and distribute them to previously prepared hiding places near the bridges. At Charles' request, several canisters of arms—pistols, rifles, and submachine guns—were dropped.

These were for the guards who would protect the people actually placing the charges on the bridges.

Now the training began to intensify. Suddenly there was a new air of urgency about the whole business. Before, it had all been on paper, abstract and remote. Now, the explosives were here. They could handle the guns, run their hands over the cold metal of the barrels, and know that now at last Lilas was a force to be reckoned with. "We'll show the Boches," they whispered to one another. And there was the other message, the talisman that gave them hope: "The invasion is coming."

Each day, the tension rose another notch, though Charles struggled to contain it. All through May, he sent small groups out into the woods to practice with the arms, to learn about explosives and detonators, to trace out the routes that they would use to get to the bridges undetected, and to work off their nervous energy. "If we don't start soon," he told Caton, "we'll all explode from sheer excitement."

"Worse than that," the doctor answered, "sooner or later, the Germans will learn about all this activity. So far, we have been lucky, but how long will that luck hold?"

On the first day of June, Charles was working in the dining room of the chateau when Armand entered, a telegram flimsy in his hand. Without a word, he handed it to Charles.

The message from London was short: "Leopard landing Field Zebra 11 P.M. June 2. He has new orders for you."

"Leopard" was Captain Peter Ivors.

4

The train from Cherbourg to Paris was four hours late arriving at the Montparnasse railroad station. The Allied air raids had intensified since the beginning of June, and the bombers had concentrated on the rail lines and bridges leading to Normandy. Rumors of invasion were rife. There was an air of excitement and worry among the passengers on the train, all of whom remembered all too vividly the horrors of the defeat by the German army in 1940. Now France was once again to be a battlefield.

Hiding his disgust, Charles listened to the complaints of the man sitting next to him in the back of the crowded car. For the past eight hours he had been treated to an unending diatribe against the Allies for the damage to the rails, for the delays, even for the food and coal shortages. It seemed that the elderly lawyer held Churchill responsible for all the miseries of life under the occupation. True, it was safer to criticize the British than the Germans, but since the fliers were risking their lives for the coming liberation of France from the Nazis, it would have been more patriotic to be silent. Frenchmen and Frenchwomen were falling every day before German firing squads . . . and this idiot complained of shortages! Besides, everyone knew that food and coal were lacking because they were sent to Germany.

Charles looked at his watch. If there were no more delays, thirty minutes more would see them in Paris. There was pleasure in that thought. He had not been in his native city since 1941. Two and a half years had passed since that terrible night when, gun in hand, he had crouched on the balcony outside Gestapo headquarters on the rue Lauriston and killed two men in as many blazing seconds. Yet the memory was as vivid as if it had been yesterday. . . . Charles shuddered, and the lawyer flattered himself that his stories had affected this sensitive young man. Encouraged, he started a new litany of horrors about the black market and the high cost of living.

With a muttered apology, Charles rose and hurried down the aisle; the lawyer would think he was going to the lavatory. Making his way through the crowded car, he pretended to lose his balance as the train clattered over another series of filled-in bomb craters and knocked against a sleeping young man slumped in his seat. Awakened so rudely from his nap, the traveler protested vociferously; Charles said something indistinct and moved on. He went through the door at the end of the car and stood on the swaying platform, waiting.

Peter Ivors came through the door two minutes later still rubbing his shoulder. "I say, Charles, you might have been a little more delicate about awakening me. This is the first sleep I've had since leaving England."

"Speak French, even when we're alone," Charles warned, "and don't look directly at me. We're supposed to be strangers, and here people don't strike up conversations on trains as easily as they do in your country."

Peter moved to the other side of the platform, lit a cigarette, and stared moodily at the passing countryside.

Last night, by feeble moonlight and with the aid of several small flares, an R.A.F. light plane had landed on a flat pasture in Normandy. It had quickly taxied up to a little knot of people, turned into the wind, and stayed just long enough to let Peter and two other agents descend from the cabin. Then, with a roar of its engine that had shaken the trees, it had rushed down the improvised runway, leaped into the air, and disappeared into the night. The flares had been extinguished and the three newcomers bundled into a small van and driven to their "safe house," the Château Vaucouleurs, where Charles had been waiting for them.

There had been no greetings; it had not been a social occasion. The new orders from London had been quite explicit: two agents were to be put on the train for Lyons, and Peter—accompanied by Charles—was to report to the chief of Allied Intelligence in Paris. The mission would be explained to Charles en route, but Peter and Charles had been cautioned not to travel together, in case of an identity check. The needless warning had irritated Charles. He was too old a hand to be caught with bad papers, and he was certain that Peter's forged identity card was another piece of the spy school's impeccable workmanship. London, he guessed, was having invasion jitters too. . . .

During the long eight-hour trip, Charles had waited for Peter to give him some sign of a meeting to explain the orders, but the young Englishman had slept the entire time.

"We'll be in Paris in about twenty-five minutes,"

Charles said now. "It's time you told me what we are to do when we arrive." There was a touch of impatience in his voice.

"Sorry, old man. It was thought best not to send these orders by radio. Never can tell what the enemy is intercepting and decoding these days. Wouldn't do to hand them the name and address of our top man in Paris. As a matter of fact, I don't have it either, but it will be waiting for us at the Montparnasse station. In any case, we are to contact him for further instructions. He wants you to brief him on the situation in the Cotentin and show him your plan for sabotage."

Charles started to protest, but Peter cut him short. "I know. All of this could have been done by courier without a dangerous train trip across France, but there is more to it than that . . . much more."

The young Englishman paused and looked back into the car to see if anyone was paying undue attention to them or was coming in their direction. No one was.

"The point is, Charles, we are very concerned about the situation in Paris. Rumors have reached us of preparations for a full-scale uprising by the French Resistance to coincide with the invasion. Now you might think that this would help our landing, and possibly it would—but think of the cost. The Allied armies don't expect to reach Paris for two months after D-Day, and in that time the Resistance uprising will be smothered in blood. In Paris there are few arms, no military organization, no trained troops. They wouldn't have a beggar's chance against the Germans. It would be a massacre."

A puff of smoke, then a long pause as Peter considered his next words carefully. "Our mission is to confirm that an insurrection is being planned, and to find out who is behind it. It is not being directed from London. No one there wants to see Paris destroyed. But there's no doubt that the destruction of Paris is what is being prepared here. Our job is to determine how this madness can be stopped."

Charles exploded. "Do you realize what you are asking? You're asking Frenchmen to do nothing to free their country from the Boches, to just sit around while the Allies fight their way to Paris and hand us our freedom on a platter! And, oh yes, we will be expected to be eternally grateful to the liberators—"

"That's not fair, Charles," Peter said quickly. "The Resistance has a vital role in the coming battle, and you know it. But not in Paris. The world would never forgive us if we allowed all that beauty to be destroyed in a hopeless attempt to free the city before our armies arrive."

Charles remembered what his father had once said: "Paris is not France, just the capital." But was it true? He did not doubt that the Nazis in their fury at the uprising would level the city, blast the lovely bridges over the Seine, crumble the glorious buildings that were so much a part of the country's history. Paris a sea of ashes with tens of thousands dead under the debris? Perhaps Peter was right. An uprising would be in the great tradition of the Parisians, in the spirit of 1870, when they had eaten rats rather than surrender to the Prussians, but it would be a useless and costly gesture.

"What are we supposed to do to prevent this uprising?" Charles asked.

"Sorry, old man, I don't have the faintest idea. My orders are to take you with me to Prosper, deliver a letter, and then take further orders from him."

Prosper was the almost legendary chief of the Allied Intelligence networks in France and Belgium, one of the handful of men who commanded the loyalty of the thousands of British, American, and French agents fighting the underground war. He was rumored to have been a don at Cambridge before the war, and there were stories of his putting on a German uniform and penetrating the closely guarded Gestapo prison at Fresnes to free two of his arrested agents. With a twinge, Charles remembered the equally legendary Max, whom he had once met on a deserted riverbank in Vichy. Max had been dead for over a year now; he had been betrayed by a comrade and tortured to death.

Majo had accompanied Charles on that mission. They had pretended to be campers, a carefree young couple out to see the countryside, heedless of the war—a young couple the Gestapo hardly need take an interest in. Charles remembered the warm sun, sitting in the park sharing fruit with Majo, the first sight of Max, and the transfer of the papers at the river's edge. There had been trouble on the trip back to Paris—the Germans had closed the border between Vichy and the north—so the two young campers had spent the night in a barn.

Now Max was dead, tortured to death by the Nazis, and Majo—the lovely Seagull—was in a German concentration camp. All these years, Charles had been afraid to think of her in that hell for fear that the thought would weaken him. He had always felt a terrible guilt that he should have escaped when the others had been arrested. But now he let Majo's image fill his mind, and he felt a renewed strength and sense of purpose. *The invasion is coming—perhaps the beginning of the end of the war. People have survived in Ravensbrück. I will find Majo again.*

Charles shook his head to clear it of ghosts. He had warned his own people not to dwell on lost comrades: "The struggle must go on. That is the only way to make certain their suffering was not in vain." But Majo was not lost. She was alive and waiting for him.

The telegraph poles were passing the train more slowly now. They were coming into Paris. In the distance, the ivory white dome of the Church of the Sacred Heart could be seen under the gray skies.

Paris—still under the boots of the Nazis.

They got off the train separately and Charles followed Peter into the crowded railroad station. There were police everywhere, checking identity cards at random, searching suitcases, or just standing around watching, looking for anything—or anyone—the least bit suspicious. Without even having to seek them out, Charles knew that Gestapo agents were also nearby, waiting to step in if an arrest was to be made.

Charles bought a newspaper and stood near the kiosk pretending to read it while Peter went to a telephone. The procedure for establishing contact with another agent was routine. In a particular telephone book on a particular page (the number of which had been given Peter before he left England), there would be one name lightly underlined. The name was not important, but the address was. At a time given by the first three digits of the telephone number, they would be met at that address and taken to the rendezvous with Prosper.

Peter came out of the telephone booth, picked up his suitcase, and walked briskly through the exit. Charles followed and caught up to him at the entrance to the subway station. There was a policeman standing at the ticket booth, but he paid no attention to the two young men who politely bought second-class tickets (only the Germans traveled first class in the metro). They found seats in different parts of the same car, and Charles, pretending to be buried in his newspaper, watched Peter for the signal that their station was the next stop.

They were ten minutes early for the rendezvous. (Prosper had obviously known that the train would be late when he'd selected the time for their meeting.) Rather than risk arousing suspicion by loitering, they walked slowly around the block staring at the buildings as if looking for a certain number. It was a working-class neighborhood—small shops, third-rate hotels, and tiny bars lined the streets. The people looked pale and anxious. It had been a hard winter, and the lack of food and fuel showed in the drained, nervous expressions on the faces of the men and women who passed by. Charles noted the long lines in front of the grocers', butchers', and bakers' shops. Women stood apathetically, hoping for a bit of meat, a few potatoes, perhaps a dab of butter for their hungry families. All too often they were disappointed.

A man came out of a bar, yelling something over his shoulder at the owner. With a broad smile, a little tipsy, he walked up to Peter and asked for a light for his cigarette. Hunched over the flame, he mumbled a few words as he puffed desperately; then, with a wave of the hand, he staggered down the street.

"Our contact?" Charles asked. Peter nodded and led the way across the street and into a dark doorway. There was a small courtyard behind the entrance, filled with the remains of what had once been a fountain and some withered shrubs. At the far end, there was a large wooden door.

Prosper's apartment was on the third floor. Charles was surprised that there were no guards in front of the headquarters of Allied Intelligence for the Paris area. It seemed disturbingly reckless.

The man who opened the door looked more like a schoolmaster than the renowned leader of a clandestine war. Medium height, slight, with bushy brown hair and bulging eyes. Through thick bifocals, Prosper looked them over distraitly, as if he had been disturbed at his work by two unexpected students. Then, without a word, he waved them in and locked the door.

"We'll talk in the dining room," Prosper said in a piping voice. "Much cozier in there. Leave your suitcases in that closet."

There was a pot of coffee—"Almost impossible to get these days," Prosper said cheerfully—and a plate of sandwiches on the dining room table. Charles realized that he was famished. They had had to skip breakfast, and there had been nothing to eat on the train.

As they devoured the food, Prosper leaned across the table and lectured them on the situation in Paris. "First of all, you should realize that the Resistance is badly split, despite Max's best efforts to unite the factions. Oh yes, there is a high council that is supposed to represent the united forces that are fighting the Germans, but the truth is that every political party controls its own Resistance group, and they don't trust one another. There is more backbiting, more spying, more quarreling over the distribution of arms and money from London than at any time since the war began. As the invasion gets closer, this will inevitably increase."

There was a knock on the door. Prosper opened it a crack and took the small envelope that was thrust through. He read its contents, whispered some order, and locked the door again. At the table, he burned the message in an ashtray, crumpled the ashes into a fine powder, then resumed his lecture.

"The largest group here in Paris is the Communist Resistance. They are the key to what is happening, and what will happen in the coming months. Ever since the Nazis attacked the Soviet Union, the Communists have been making armed attacks on the occupation troops without any thought of what the consequences might be. After the first attack, the Germans took hostages. After the second Nazi officer was shot dead, they started shooting these innocent men in reprisal. Thousands have fallen before German firing squads to avenge a handful of murdered Germans—almost a hundred Frenchmen for each Nazi. It's crazy, but the Communists won't listen to any arguments—they've been killing Nazi officers for three years now. Mind you, many of the hostages were members of their own party, but even that doesn't deter them. They keep talking about 'the blood of martyrs,' and they claim that the shooting of hostages will pull France from its present lethargy and swell the ranks of the Resistance."

"And has it?" Peter asked.

The question was logical, but Charles thought it in bad taste. *I couldn't recruit over the bodies of executed hostages,* he thought. *I see Frenchmen crumpling before the volleys of German firing squads in the ditches at Vincennes. But then Peter and Prosper are English; they see only the mission.*

"Hard to tell," Prosper said thoughtfully. "Since the German defeats began—Stalingrad, North Africa, Sicily, Italy—the mood of the people is more and more pro-Allied, but the majority still sit on the fence waiting to see if these secret weapons that Hitler boasts of won't change the tide of the war. Yes, we have more volunteers now, and I understand that the important French bankers and industrialists who were such ardent supporters of Vichy are now hedging their bets by feeding money to the Resistance—even to the Communists!"

"What about these rumors of an uprising in Paris to free the city before the Allies arrive?" Peter's voice was impatient, and Prosper smiled wanly at the implied rebuke.

"Not just rumors anymore. There are arms cached in a hundred places around Paris. The Communists have their own army—they call them *Franc-Tireurs et Partisans*—maybe two or three thousand well-disciplined men ready to take to the barricades at the signal. In addition, the Communists have gained a lot of influence with the other Resistance groups, who admire the way they shoot down Germans in the streets. I don't doubt that if and when Duclos gives the order—"

Charles interrupted. "Jacques Duclos? He's here in Paris?"

The other two men looked at him curiously. Prosper twiddled the spoon in his coffee cup before answering. "We know for a certainty that Duclos is directing the whole operation, but not from Paris. As a former deputy in the National Assembly, he is too well known here. No, Duclos is hiding out close by in the country. His second-in-command is running the show here, a man by the name of Emile Labru. I was told that one of you knows him."

"I know him," Charles said. "We worked together here in Paris some years ago . . . the Vidal–Kléber network. Labru belonged to a Communist Resistance group that cooperated with us. He's a good man." He felt as if he were still defending his friend before a board of British officers; he heard his voice becoming defiant.

Prosper put down his cup and saucer. It was clear that what he was about to say was distasteful to him.

"Your orders—and they come from London, not from me—are to contact Labru, gain his confidence, and find out what you can about the plans for this uprising in Paris. How many men he has, how many guns and of what type, and where and when they will strike."

Charles could feel the hot flush of anger in his cheeks, and his right hand was trembling with rage, but he choked off the indignant refusal that rattled in his throat. He was a soldier and the son of a French officer—the product of a long line of military men. He had learned discipline at a very tender age. Besides, the embarrassed look on Prosper's face and the hangdog expression on Peter's took some of the humiliation out of the orders. They did not like it any more than he. But they too were soldiers.

Forcing himself to relax in his chair, Charles thought the situation out for several minutes before he spoke. "I know that I am a spy, trained, equipped, and dropped into France as a spy, but do I have to spy on an old friend who is on our side in this battle?"

"Charles," Peter said pleadingly. "The Germans have ten thousand troops in Paris, and they can summon twenty thousand in a few hours from nearby garrisons. They have tanks, machine guns, flamethrowers, planes. . . . Labru has a handful of men and some obsolete rifles, maybe a few grenades. He doesn't have a chance, and if he tries, the Nazis in their fury will destroy Paris. Yes, leave it a field of ashes. We know that Hitler has ordered this destruction of the city if the Resistance takes to the barricades."

In any case, Charles thought, *it will do no harm to talk to Labru—about the old days. Perhaps he has some news of Majo . . . perhaps she has been released . . .*

With a deep sigh, he slumped wearily in his chair. "How do I find Labru?"

"You don't," Prosper said. "He's in hiding, but will get in touch with you. That message I received earlier—the one I burned—said you were to be at the falcon's nest at exactly four this afternoon. I assume you know where that is, because it means nothing to me."

Charles smiled wanly. "I know where it is," he said, but he offered no explanation. Instead, he began his report on his sabotage plan for the isolation of the Cotentin peninsula: how many pounds of high explosives would be required to blow this bridge, that section of railroad track; how many men would be needed at what position. . . .

He could see that Prosper was annoyed at his secrecy, but he preferred that Prosper and Peter Ivors not know where he would be meeting Labru. Until proven otherwise, Labru was still a friend, a comrade in this filthy war.

It was shortly after three o'clock when Charles left the apartment. Some changes had been suggested in the sabotage plan, and Charles had been given last-minute instructions about telephoning after he had met Labru. Prosper's handshake had shown that he was still irritated with Charles. Peter had been warmer in his farewell.

Charles walked rapidly down the street past the shops with their empty windows. The Germans had bought everything in sight and had requisitioned the output of the factories, so for years the counters had been vacant.

Every so often Charles glanced quickly behind him or studied the reflection of the street in the shop windows. It took him a while, for the street was crowded, but he eventually spotted the man following him: short, with a round face and a broad mustache, dressed in a yellow polo shirt and blue slacks.

At the street corner, Charles knelt suddenly and fumbled with his shoelace. Glancing backward, he saw that his "tail" had also stopped short and was studying an empty shop window as if it were filled with luxury items. Charles smiled to himself. *So Prosper wants to know where the rendezvous will be . . . and then probably to have Labru followed to his hideout.* Well, Charles was not about to be so accommodating.

A subway entrance was just around the corner. Charles walked quickly down the stairs, bought a ticket, and hurried down the tunnel to the platform. He did not have to turn again to know that his shadow was not far behind.

When the train came rumbling noisily into the station, Charles waited politely until three young nuns, two elderly men, and the man in the yellow polo shirt had entered the last car; then he followed and stood uncertainly next to the door. Out of the corner of his eye, he could see the "shadow" taking a seat farther down the car. An elderly gentleman pointed out an empty seat, but Charles smiled and shook his head. He looked about the car as if searching for someone, but all the time he was listening intently. He tensed his muscles. He was ready.

With a loud hiss of air, the doors behind him began to close. At the last minute, Charles grabbed the edge of the closing door and squeezed out onto the platform. The doors closed behind him. He could see the "shadow" half rise in his seat, but it was too late. The train started off, and Charles was left alone on the platform.

Good-bye, my friend, he thought gleefully as the train disappeared down the tunnel. *Try explaining to Prosper how you were fooled by the oldest trick in the book.*

He went through the exit, climbed the stairs, and crossed the tracks to catch a train going in the opposite direction. This time no one followed him. Prosper had been overconfident; there was no backup for the "tail."

Forty minutes later, he reached the rendezvous, a shabby third-rate hotel on a back street in the University quarter. It was here that he had hidden out after shooting the turncoat radio operator and the Gestapo officer. Labru had named it during one of his daily visits with food and information: "Since you are called Falcon, then this must be your nest." After three years, the hotel was still badly in need of a coat of paint, and its windows seemed dirtier than ever.

In the semi-gloom of the lobby, watched by two young men playing cards, Charles walked to the reception desk. The clerk took a wooden match out of his mouth and stared expectantly.

"Falcon," Charles said quietly. The two guards relaxed and went back to their game.

"Up those stairs," the clerk said, jerking a thumb at the back of the lobby. "He's expecting you." He pressed a button underneath the counter to warn listeners upstairs that Falcon was coming.

On the first-floor landing, a young man dressed in a tan jacket and dark trousers watched Charles come up the stairs; then he knocked twice, slowly, on the door of room

108. Without waiting for an answer, he opened the door, and stepped aside to allow Charles to enter.

Labru rose from behind a table covered with papers, files, and maps. He came forward, a smile on his face, and embraced Charles. Then he stepped back and looked shrewdly at him. "You've changed, Falcon. You're taller, and the baby fat is all gone. You look fit enough. Are you still the tough guy who told Duclos off when he didn't think you could do the job on Pascal?"

"You've changed too, Labru," Charles said with a grin. "A little more weight, a few more gray hairs—very distinguished, I must say—even a bourgeois necktie and business suit. What happened to the bartender of the Café Denis?"

"Gone, my friend, gone. We're very respectable now. The whole Resistance looks up to us, even those who don't share our political beliefs. We can't go around looking like anarchist bomb throwers, can we? What would all those conservative army officers and shopkeepers think of us?" Labru motioned to an armchair and sat down behind the cluttered table. "Look at this! Reports, accounts, assignments, operations . . . would you believe that they have me pushing a pencil behind a desk? Me, Labru, who ran the toughest action squad in the Paris Resistance!"

Charles smiled at the image of his friend as a harried executive. Then the smile faded. It was time to be honest with Labru.

"You know why I'm here," Charles began. "The British and Americans are very worried about an uprising in Paris before their troops arrive. They say it will be a massacre of the Resistance, and would mean the total destruction of the city. They asked me to talk you out of any such idea."

There was a long silence. Labru frowned and fiddled with some papers on the table. "I appreciate your frankness, Falcon. Not that I expected anything less from you; we're old friends and should be open with each other. But this business is not going to be decided by you, me, the Americans, or the British. It is the temper and the spirit of the people of Paris that will decide whether they will accept their freedom as a gift from the Allies, or willingly spill their blood in the streets to gain it for themselves. I don't have to remind you of the tradition of the barricades, the revolutionary tradition of the men and women who stormed the Bastille; beheaded a king; overthrew the government in 1789, 1830, and 1848; said no to the abject surrender by the politicians to the Prussians in 1870; and formed their own government—the Commune—which was drowned in blood by the Vichyites of that day."

"I know my French history," Charles said coldly. "But the last time the Parisians tried against frightful odds to liberate their city was seventy-five years ago—and they failed! Think of what will happen if you send your men, with the few arms they have, against well-equipped, well-trained German soldiers. They won't have a chance! Hitler has sworn to reduce Paris to ashes if we resist, and you know that it will be done. What would be the point of liberating ruins . . . or a cemetery?"

"Pride, national unity through the common struggle against the enemy, a new spirit that will raise France—"

Charles cut off the words with a wave of his hand. "Spare me the slogans of your Central Committee." Labru stiffened at the sarcasm. His eyes narrowed, and there was a tightness about his mouth. *I'd better be careful,* Charles thought, *or all this will end badly.* "Sorry, Labru. I had no right to say that. I know that the Communists have been in the forefront of the armed struggle against the Boches, but I also remember that—except for a few men like you whose patriotism was stronger than their politics—the Communists waited until the Nazis attacked the Soviet Union before joining us in the fight."

"And I was one of the few who fought from the first hour."

"I know that, and that is why we are friends, but what you plan now is madness, insanity. It makes sense only if you're hoping to use it as a springboard to power. Does your Central Committee think that an uprising, even if it fails, will give it such prestige that a grateful people will carry the party to power after the liberation?"

The older man bristled with indignation. "I know nothing of that. I carry out orders and leave to others the responsibility for the consequences."

Charles rose and leaned across the table until they were face to face. "I carry out orders too, Labru. Right now I am getting ready to blow up a number of bridges—never mind where. As a result of those orders, many of the peasants and townspeople in the area will suffer. Some will die either in the explosions or by Nazi reprisals. *But it is absolutely essential that those bridges be destroyed.* The lives of thousands of troops, the success of the invasion, depend upon it. Otherwise I could never do what I must do."

Charles paused for breath. Labru was still stony-faced, but a little nerve in his left cheek was twitching.

"Tomorrow," Charles continued, "I want you to go down to the Seine. Walk across one of those lovely bridges that are the city's pride; look about you at the magnificent buildings that are our heritage, our tradition, and our gift of beauty to the world. Then ask yourself if you really have the right to crumble those bridges into the river, to burn those buildings—to destroy our most precious wealth, the riches our children have the right to inherit. Can you do this for empty words? For a pride that will not accept liberation from our allies, who will be risking their lives to free us?"

Charles straightened, turned, and walked to the door. Standing in the open doorway, he looked back for an answer. Labru lowered his eyes and stared sullenly at his papers.

It was then that Charles knew he had failed.

At the corner bar, Charles dialed the number that Prosper had given him. An unfamiliar voice answered, but gave the correct code response. Before Charles could report, the voice said excitedly, "Auntie has been seized by a new attack. The situation is critical. You had better hurry if you want to be in time!"

Putting down the receiver with exquisite care, Charles glanced about him as casually as he could, his heart pounding. The code message was clear: the countess had been arrested and he was to return to Normandy at once.

5

"Luckily our guards were alert," Caton said, gripping the steering wheel more tightly. "They spotted the strange truck with the large antenna loop on the top as it turned toward the chateau at the crossroads."

Slumped wearily next to him, Charles stared out at the passing scene. He had been on the train for ten hours, and, when the doctor had picked him up at six A.M. in front of the Cherbourg station, he had been without sleep for almost thirty hours. In spite of his exhaustion, he tried to concentrate on Caton's story. It was vital to know how bad the damage was. In the back seat, Louise watched the road behind them to see if they were being followed.

"Armand had just enough time to crawl through the 'rathole' and close the opening with the box before the Germans rushed through the front door," Caton went on. "The countess tried to delay them, but they pushed her aside and ran through the rooms, pistols in hand. They moved all the large pieces of furniture, tore down the drapes, tapped the walls, and threatened poor Emilie. They searched the attic, but they didn't move the box. I guess they were too tired by that time to move all the furniture and junk we had piled up to conceal the radio room. After all, there were only four of them. But they found an eighteenth-century fowling piece, so rather than look foolish by returning empty-handed, they arrested the countess for illegal possession of arms."

"Emilie?"

"They let her go. She is staying with relatives in town."

"And Armand?"

Caton shook his head in disbelief. "It was astonishing. The Germans left with the countess about one P.M. and it was after two when Emilie's nephew reached me with the news. According to Emilie, Armand had sprinted for the radio room as soon as the alarm was given. The Germans had left two guards at the chateau—one at the front door and one at the back door—so poor Armand was trapped in the attic . . . with our only radio.

"At midnight, eight of us were at Leclair's farm getting ready to attack the chateau and rescue Armand and the radio. I had telephoned our man in Paris and told him to find you at Prosper's with the news, but I didn't think we could wait for you to return. Any hour now the Germans might go back to the chateau and start a real search. If they moved the furniture and junk in the attic, Armand was lost, so we had to act soon. We had guns now, so we were going to attack just before dawn, kill the guards, and rescue Armand.

"A little before one o'clock, just as we finished planning the attack, the door opens and in walks Armand, cool as a cucumber, carrying the radio in an old suitcase he had found in the attic. Not a word did he say about how he got past the guards and out of the chateau. He asked if we had any news of the countess, whether you had been contacted, and did we mind if he set up the radio in the bedroom because there was no electricity in the barn."

Charles stifled a grin at the doctor's wondering tone. *Caton has no idea what went on*, he thought. "I feel sorry for the guards," he said aloud.

Caton took his eyes from the road long enough to see if Charles was joking. "You feel sorry for the Germans who had Armand trapped in the attic?"

"Yes, indeed. You've never had the opportunity to see Armand operate with a knife, so you can't appreciate how helpless those guards were. He gave a demonstration one day for the students at the spy school. There were nine of us in a large room lit only by faint moonlight filtering through the curtains, and we could barely see one another. We were told to listen, and to yell when we heard a menacing noise. Then Armand crept into the room. He stalked us one by one, and we heard nothing. The first indication we had that he was close was the dull edge of his blade at our throats. So you see, those two Germans were sitting ducks."

That night at Leclair's farm, Charles sat at the scrubbed wooden table with Caton and an elderly storekeeper named Bousquet. For an hour they had been engaged in a heated discussion. Charles had urged that immediate plans be made to rescue the countess. He had argued that the rescue attempt was necessary for the morale of Lilas. Otherwise, the members of the group would feel that if they ever fell into the hands of the Gestapo, their situation would be hopeless. Caton had listened gloomily, now and then pointing out the dangers of any rescue attempt. "We would almost certainly be captured or killed," Caton had said. "That is why we didn't try to rescue Titus and the others."

It was precisely because nothing could be done for Titus and the others that they must try to rescue the countess, Charles had insisted. Bousquet, who ran the Cherbourg network, had been silent most of the time, watching the red-faced young Marceau and the pale doctor. . . .

"We can't storm Gestapo headquarters in Cherbourg," Charles now said bitterly. "It's a fortress, and we've too few men and arms. It will have to be while she is being moved. A woman of the countess's position won't be left in the hands of anyone but the Paris Gestapo. No, they'll send her to Paris soon. Will it be possible to get advance notice of this move, Bousquet?"

The old man grunted and nodded his head. "There is a fellow who runs the local black market for the Gestapo in Cherbourg. He spends a lot of time in their headquarters on business matters. Well, lately he has started to worry about the Germans' losing the war, so he contacted us and offered his services as a 'patriotic' Frenchman. I'll get word to him that we want news of the countess."

"I should think they would take her in a car," Charles said.

"No doubt about it," Bousquet agreed. "Probably two or three cars, with maybe ten or twelve guards, all heavily armed." There was a solemn pause; then the old man continued. "You know, of course, that if the Germans think a successful rescue is likely, they will immediately shoot the countess."

Suddenly, Charles could not bear to sit there any longer, coolly analyzing the pros and cons. He got up abruptly and walked to the window, trying to understand the powerful emotions that had seized him. Of course the countess's life would be in jeopardy; surely he had been aware of that all along. But he had to go through with this rescue. He was prepared to disregard or to overcome any danger, no matter how great. . . .

He realized he was thinking like a fanatic, an amateur, not like the trained head of an underground network who was responsible for many lives. And then he remembered the last time he had thought this way. When Majo had been taken by the Nazis, he had been prepared to take any risk, make any sacrifice, to free her; but he had been persuaded by Labru that it was impossible. And perhaps his own fear had added weight to Labru's arguments. Was it guilt about having left Majo in enemy hands that made him so blindly determined to rescue the countess? Was he justified in pursuing a course that—militarily—was the height of folly, perhaps even risking the success of the Allied invasion, in order to assuage his own emotional distress? Charles stood gripping the window frame, peering out across the dark fields toward the road, where Leclair and Alain stood guard. It was better that Bousquet and Caton did not see his face just now.

The door creaked and Charles turned as Armand came into the room, a broad grin on his swarthy face. The radio operator murmured a soft greeting to the three men, reached into his shirt pocket, took out a yellow message form, and dropped it casually on the table. "I've just finished decoding this. It's marked priority one, so it must be important."

Charles walked back to the table, picked up the yellow sheet, read it, then read it again and sighed deeply. His decision had been made—by others, miles from where he stood.

"We can stop quarreling about the rescue," he said. "There will be no rescue. In fact, there will be no transfer of the countess to Paris. By tomorrow, nothing moves in or out of the Cotentin."

Caton leaped to his feet, delight on his face. "The invasion!"

Charles nodded. "This is the code word to start the sabotage. The landings begin within twenty-four hours, starting from noon today."

The floor of the woods was covered with the moldy undergrowth of several seasons, and the early evening rain had made the ground slippery. As they made their way through the darkness, the members of the team began to tire under their heavy loads. Someone cried out in pain, and Charles hurried back along the file to find a man with a twisted ankle writhing on the ground. Charles did what he could—he wrapped a bandage tightly around the man's ankle, propped him against a tree, and then left him. This was not a soccer game; there were no time-outs for injuries. One gone still left fifteen to do this job.

They reached the railroad bridge near St. Sauveur le Vicomte just after midnight and swiftly went to work. No order had to be given, no word spoken. Time and again Charles had rehearsed them for this task, making each man and woman explain on a scale drawing of the bridge exactly what his or her job would be: "With Paul, I will go to the third girder from the opposite bank and attach six blocks of explosive at the point where it joins this strut. . . ." At the last review, there had been mumbles of discontent at the repetition, but Charles had cut the complaining short. "One mistake and we'll all be blown into the river," he had reminded them.

Armand had calculated the points where the explosives were to be placed, and the amounts to be used. As he hurried to his position and began strapping the gray blocks to a girder, Charles prayed silently that the radio operator knew his business. If he had miscalculated, there would be a spectacular explosion, but the bridge would not fall and would be easily repaired by the Germans.

"Hand me the fuses and wire," he whispered to Louise. She reached into the knapsack and pulled out the detonating charges. Charles noted with approval that she was working efficiently.

Crimping the fuses to the wires with a pair of pliers was awkward in the darkness; Charles focused all his attention on working quickly, but not hastily. As he was inserting the last fuse into the explosive block, he heard a high-pitched birdcall from one of the guards. It was the danger signal. Someone was coming!

Clutching the roll of wire against his chest, Charles leaned back into the protecting darkness under the bridge. Louise swiftly climbed up and straddled the strut above him. Although Charles could not see the others, he knew that they too were motionless at their positions. All this had been planned for. They would remain unseen unless someone flashed a light under the bridge.

Holding his breath, Charles clung to the girder. It could not have been more than a minute, but it seemed like hours before he heard the rumbling of a railroad handcart on the roadbed above: a patrol, inspecting the tracks. *So the enemy is nervous too,* Charles thought.

The sound of the handcart passed overhead, then receded. For one heart-stopping minute, Charles imagined he heard the handcart reverse, as if the patrol suspected something, but he was wrong. Soon it was still again, and they went back to work.

The position of each fuse was checked and the lead-in wires taped to the nearest girder so that they could not be pulled loose. The ends of the wires from one fuse were spliced to those at the next point, and so on down the line. Charles and Louise carefully unrolled the final set of wires as they backed off away from the bridge, along the bank, then up a slope to where the detonator had been placed. The other workers, following their instructions, had already gathered there.

Armand came up the slope, knelt beside them, and whispered, "I've checked. It all looks fine." He scraped the ends of the two wires to expose the copper centers and attached them to the firing pins of the detonator box.

This was the moment they had all worked and prayed for, the end of all the training and planning. Although he could barely make out the faces of the men and women clustered around him, Charles could sense their excitement. He lifted the plunger handle and paused. Glancing at Louise, he smiled almost gaily.

Now!

The plunger handle slammed down, closing the circuit between the battery and the wires.

There was a brilliant white flash, then a roar as the shock wave swept over them. Explosion followed explosion all along the bridge, outlining its dark framework against globes of red and orange light. Fountains of spray leaped from the river and a wall of smoke rolled outward and overflowed the banks.

For one terrible second Charles thought that they had failed, as the bridge quivered but did not move. Armand cursed under his breath. Then there was another, final explosion. The far end of the bridge lifted and twisted. In four separate sections, the bridge collapsed and plunged into the river. There was a booming roar as it smashed into the water, whipping up the dark surface. Awe-stricken, the little group of saboteurs stared down at the twisted remains still clinging to the stone piers. Carried away by the excitement, Louise clapped her hands and shouted, "Bravo!" Armand kissed her cheek.

It was done. The bridge was gone. With luck, the other

three groups had been as successful and all four bridges had been destroyed.

Charles threw the detonator box into the bushes. "Let's go," he ordered. "The Germans will know that wasn't just a truck backfiring." They melted into the darkness and began the dangerous trip back.

Everyone was exultant. No German train would cross the river for a month. What a sight it had been . . . their first bridge! They whispered gleefully to one another until Charles gruffly ordered silence.

An hour later, they were halfway to their destination, still deep in the dark forest, when they heard the distant sounds of antiaircraft fire. As they passed through a clearing, they could see the pinpoints of light dotting the sky to the north.

"An air raid on Cherbourg?" a voice asked timidly.

"No," Charles said, "we would have heard the sounds of bombs even at this distance. Probably some fighter planes passing through on their way to strafe German installations around Paris."

Five minutes later, there was a deep droning sound. At first no one could recognize it, and almost instinctively they drew closer together, as if to protect one another. Finally, as the sound deepened, someone realized that they were hearing airplanes approaching from the north. But, perplexingly, the planes were flying very low and very slowly, so they were neither bombers nor fighters. Charles sensed the new wave of nervousness that was running through his group.

Suddenly, a large dark object crashed through the branches of a tree in front of them. Like a marionette dangling by its strings, the helmeted figure in field jacket, jump pants, and boots swung slowly, cursing with an unmistakable American accent. Another crashing sound, and Charles turned as a second black doll dropped to the ground beside him. Even as he began to understand what he was seeing, parachutists came dropping out of the sky all around them, some landing in the clearing, some getting caught in the trees, a few being dragged along the ground as the wind picked up. Twenty, thirty—it was impossible to count.

It was the first wave of the invasion! The U.S. airborne army had arrived in France!

But Charles' joy and exhilaration quickly gave way to dismay. The situation was dangerous. This unexpected encounter with the paratroopers in the dark gave neither group a way to establish contact, to determine that the other group was friendly. To the paratroopers, the small group of saboteurs vaguely seen in the darkness must be assumed to be a hostile armed force. Already some of them had taken up positions around the edge of the clearing, their rifles and submachine guns pointing toward Charles and the others. Nervous fingers were undoubtedly caressing the triggers. Any minute now, a shot would ring out—and then there would be a general exchange of fire, the tragedy of ally fighting ally.

Only a few minutes had passed since the first paratrooper had crashed down in front of them, but the tension was reaching an unbearable point. Charles knew that something had to be done immediately to let the airborne soldiers know that his group was friendly.

There wasn't time to think, so he acted without thinking. Waving his arms above his head, he shouted frantically, "Pittsburgh!"

The dark shadows around them froze. Clearly the last thing they had expected to hear in a strange French field was a shout of "Pittsburgh!" from what they thought was the enemy. They hesitated. Then one figure came forward from the edge of the clearing and approached Charles. On the front of his helmet was the single white stripe of a lieutenant. The flap of his gun holster was open and his right hand rested on the butt of his Colt automatic. He was taking no chances on this being a trap.

"What about Pittsburgh?" the lieutenant demanded fiercely.

Charles lowered his hands and grinned. "My mother is from Pittsburgh," he said. "I couldn't think of anything else that would keep you from firing. My name is Marceau, and I'm the head of this group of Resistance people. We've just blown the bridges across the Douve River. Who are you?"

The lieutenant took off his helmet and wiped his brow with his hand. "We're part of the U.S. 101st Airborne." He looked around, puzzled. "There were supposed to be over five hundred of us dropped at this point, and I can't count but thirty or forty of my men within shouting distance. Something has really gone wrong. Okay, mister. You speak damned good American, so maybe you do have an American mother. But can you prove you're French Resistance?"

His hand never left his gun butt while he spoke, and Charles could see him scanning the small group of Lilas people.

"Lieutenant, if you were a secret agent operating in enemy territory, would you carry your true identification papers on you for the Germans to find?"

The lieutenant thought this over for a moment. "We weren't told anything about Resistance people blowing up bridges in our area."

"Maybe you're not in your area," Charles suggested. "Where were you supposed to drop?"

"About three miles east of Ste. Mère Eglise."

"You are about twelve miles from your drop zone," Charles said. "Here, let me show you." He took a map from the breast pocket of his jacket and shone a small flashlight on it. "See, here's the river, and here is Ste. Mère Eglise. You should have been up there, and you're actually down here, right in the middle of these woods."

The lieutenant examined the map and then cursed softly under his breath. "Now ain't that a hell of a thing. Twelve miles off course. Wait till I see that navigator again!"

"He's worse than the one I had," Charles said. "I was dropped only five miles off target. But let's not waste time cursing the Air Force. You have to get to the rendezvous, and you'll never get there without a guide. There are too many Germans between here and there. You'll have to stay off the main road if you want to avoid them, and all these forest paths look alike in the dark. Luckily, I know these woods. So, shall we be on our way?"

The lieutenant eyed him suspiciously. "How do I know you won't lead us right into an ambush?"

"You don't," Charles said. "On the other hand, you don't have much of a choice. It's either follow me or blunder around all night and take a chance on running smack into a German patrol. If you're smart, you'll assume that I'm friendly—at least until I give some indication to the contrary. Besides, you've got guns and I'll be right at your side. At the first sign of treachery—"

"You're right. I don't have much of a choice. Any guy crazy enough to stand up in front of us and yell 'Pittsburgh' is either a nut or someone who didn't want us shooting at each other. So I'll be putting myself in the hands of either a screwball or an ally. In this war, there's not too much difference."

"Let's get started," Charles said. "It will be light soon." He turned and spoke briefly to Armand. He handed the group over to the radio operator, and reminded him of the need to disperse before reaching Leclair's farm. "We don't want the Germans alerted, although with all these paratroopers dropping down all over the place, it probably won't make too much difference." They shook hands solemnly and then Armand led his team off into the night.

The lieutenant had gathered his bewildered troopers, a few of whom were limping from sprained ankles. One of them was being supported by two comrades.

"We're ready," the lieutenant said.

Charles nodded toward the north end of the clearing. "We'll go that way. Single file and no noise. If I do this—" he flung his hands out sharply to the sides—"duck into the bushes on both sides of the path and be absolutely quiet. Let's go."

The assembly point for the American soldiers was a large vineyard dominated by a gray stone church set on a small hill. The steeple of the church could be seen for several miles, and made the rendezvous easy to find as soon as it was light.

As Charles led his little group of paratroopers out of the woods and down the dusty road to the church, he noted with dismay the confusion, almost chaos, in the vineyard. Soldiers in baggy jump pants and combat jackets were running around looking for their officers; officers were asking for orders; some men were digging foxholes, but most seemed to be wandering around aimlessly, as if lost. A hospital tent had been set up behind the church, and next to it a row of blanket-covered bodies was aligned in the sun. *Even before meeting the enemy,* Charles thought sadly. *Killed by faulty chutes or drowned in the marshes—close by, too, or they would have been left where they died until the battle was over.*

The lieutenant came out of the church with a burly major, who shook Charles' hand and then tried to explain the situation. It was clear that the air drop had been a fiasco—"the biggest foul-up in the history of warfare," the major called it. Two airborne divisions had been scattered over the Cotentin peninsula. An unexpected cloud bank had forced the planes to swerve off course, and very few had reached the drop zones assigned to them. Even now, an hour after first light, less than one-third of the force was available for the two critical missions: covering the approaches to Utah Beach, where the sea landing would soon begin, and securing Ste. Mère Eglise, a vital road junction.

"Look," the major said to Charles. "More of our men are wandering around out there unable to find the rendez-vous. Can you help them? Can your people find them and guide them to this point?"

Charles shrugged his shoulders. "We'll try, of course, but it won't be easy. Everyone is jittery and likely to fire at the slightest sound. Also, only one of my people speaks English, and it will be hard to show that we are friendly. You'd better give us the password, or we'll have them shooting at each other."

"The challenge is 'Bull' and the countersign is 'Run,' and that holds good until midnight tonight."

A man came slowly out of the church holding a map and speaking firmly to a small group of officers surrounding him. He wore no insignia, but there was about him the unmistakable air of command. At a distance, one would have taken him for just another soldier, one of the hundreds dressed in jump pants, boots, and field jackets. The only thing that set him apart was a single yellow-painted grenade attached to the webbing of his knapsack. He even had a rifle slung on one shoulder to make it more difficult for an enemy sniper to pick him out. "The Old Man," the lieutenant whispered to Charles. "The general always jumps with the first wave."

The major went up to the crag-faced general and whispered something in his ear, jerking his head toward Charles at the same time. A few words were exchanged; then the major motioned Charles forward.

"Son, I'm General Ridgway," the man wearing the yellow grenade said. "I'm in command of this mob. Most of my men are out there somewhere trying to find me. Major Dennis tells me that you run the Resistance in this area and that you're willing to help round up our people. Anything you can do would be greatly appreciated."

"We'll do our best, general."

"They tell me you're from Pittsburgh." There was an amused smile on the general's lips.

"No sir. My mother was born there. My father is a French army officer in Leclerc's armored division. I'm Lieutenant Charles Marceau, Free French Intelligence on temporary duty with the British."

General Ridgway sighed and pointed to the mass of paratroopers huddled together in the nearby fields. "This is a real mess, Marceau. If I don't get this division together as a fighting unit soon, our men will land on Utah Beach without any cover. The only exits from that beach are five causeways across flooded ground. If the

Germans hold those roads, our troops will be caught on the beach and slaughtered. Do what you can, son. It's a critical situation."

Charles saluted and started to walk away. Then he turned back and said, "General, I have a request to make."

Ridgway's eyes narrowed and he looked grim. Clearly he did not look favorably on bargaining over the safety of his men and the success of his mission. "Well?"

"After you clear the causeways and get the men off the beach, no doubt you'll be heading for Cherbourg. There is an elderly lady being held at Gestapo headquarters there—the Countess de Vaucouleurs. She is one of our group, arrested a few days ago, and we're worried about her."

The general relaxed. "I understand. Gestapo headquarters will be our first order of business when we get to Cherbourg. We'll take care of the lady. . . . Major Dennis will provide you with transportation. You'd better get started." He turned back to the group of officers and ordered them to assemble their men and move to the beach.

The jeep in which Charles was driven to Leclair's farm had been pulled from a wrecked glider only an hour before. The driver, a gangly redhead from Ohio, chewed gum furiously as he described the crash landing in the dark. "Couldn't see anything except the exhaust flames from the towplane's engines. Black, I mean it was pitch black. Bang goes the towrope release, and all the wind noises drop down to a soft sighing, and still we can't see the ground. Let me tell you, lieutenant, there were six heartfelt prayers going on in that matchbox they call a glider. I was sitting right here behind the wheel of the jeep. . . ."

A military policeman signaled them onto the main road and the redheaded private shifted gears and drove down the tree-lined macadam.

"The first thing I heard was the rumble of the glider wheels as we touched down. I could feel the damn thing slow down and I relaxed and said to myself, 'We made it.' Then suddenly everything broke apart. I never heard such a sound of splintering wood. The windshield just disappeared; one of the wing struts came through the side and almost speared me. The glider stopped, and when we crawled out I saw that the fuselage had gone between two trees at the end of this little field. The impact on the wings had saved us. The only casualty was the glider pilot—he had a broken ankle. Talk about damn fool luck."

Charles remembered the covered bodies next to the church. *Some of the glider infantry were not so lucky*, he thought grimly. It was an insane lottery: if you drew one number, you crawled out of a crashed glider unhurt; if you drew another, you hit the trees nose on and no one came out. Or the wind dragged your chute into deep water and you were pulled under by the weight you were carrying. Just crazy chance—you lived or you died.

As they sped around a bend in the road, the driver suddenly braked sharply and pulled the jeep to the side. Fifty yards ahead, two prone paratroopers were frantically signaling them to stop, pointing their rifles to the fields on the left.

Charles ducked and slid out of his seat into the ditch that paralleled the road; he was closely followed by the driver, who had paused just long enough to grab his rifle from the back seat. They huddled against the protecting slope, listening and breathing heavily.

There was an ominous silence for several minutes. Then they heard the sound of boots running across the road above them. Someone yelled an indistinct order, and there was a burst of rifle fire followed by the chatter of a light machine gun.

Charles crawled to the top of the ditch and peered cautiously down the road. Where the two paratroopers had been, a three-man machine gun crew was firing across the fields toward the far hedgerows. There was a lot of smoke and dust; through it, he could vaguely see twenty or more Airborne soldiers moving forward. As he watched, one of the shadowy figures fell. Although he could not hear it above the pounding of the machine gun, he knew that the enemy was firing back.

His heart beating violently, Charles watched his first combat. It was the blindness of the fighting that astonished him most. Not once did he see a German. Little fingers of flame would spurt out from behind a hedgerow and there would be the whine of bullets passing overhead . . . the rat-tat-tat of a machine gun would answer . . . grenades exploded with a loud *crump* . . . and then there was silence as the enemy withdrew. As the Americans moved off in pursuit, Charles and the driver crawled out of the ditch, climbed silently into the jeep, and drove away.

Armand, Caton, and Leclair were at the farm. Charles wasted no time with explanations, but quickly gave his orders. Everyone in the Lilas network was to spread out and try to find the missing paratroopers. He showed the position of the church on the map and emphasized the password. "Bull—Run. Bull—Run," he said slowly in English. "Our people must shout 'Bull,' and if the soldiers answer 'Run,' they are Americans. Don't get too close before you are recognized. Remember, these men will be edgy and trigger-happy. I am going to give you a message to show them. It may help."

On a sheet of paper, he wrote: *We are French Resistance fighters aiding General Ridgway. Follow us and we will take you to the rendezvous.*

"Make copies of this and give one to each of our people. Caton, take charge of the search in the sector north of here. Leclair and I will work the south. Armand, you and Alain pick three groups of three and fan out to the west. The paratroopers are already moving eastward to the beach, so they will pick up any strays to the east. Is everything understood? Good, let's get started. Time is short."

For hours, Charles and Leclair searched the countryside for the lost paratroopers. Everywhere there were small groups of them—five, ten, seldom more—wandering helplessly about looking for a landmark. Their relief at finding someone who spoke English was obvious, and they readily accepted Charles' offer to guide them. Soon the group behind him was a hundred strong, and it was time to turn back to the church. Only once did the enemy fire at them, and then a quick fusillade persuaded the Germans to leave them alone.

It was a grim journey. As they passed through the woods, they saw the bodies of paratroopers who had drowned in the swamps, weighted down by their heavy packs. Here and there the crumpled, torn remains of gliders, one with a jeep pushed halfway through the side, showed among the trees. Landing at night without lights had been fatal to crews and passengers. Charles peered into the cockpit of one glider to see if anyone was alive, and was horrified to see a bloody face staring back with sightless eyes. Shuddering, he returned to the column and led them quickly away.

The fields around the church were empty, and only a skeleton staff remained to sort out the newcomers and send them after the others. In the distance could be heard the crackle of small-arms fire as General Ridgway led his fragmented division into battle for the causeways. There was a muffled, deep-throated roar, and Charles looked inquiringly at Major Dennis.

"Naval gunfire. They're covering the landings on the beach."

Charles sent Leclair back to resume the search. He picked up a rifle from a pile in front of the church and examined it carefully. As if reading his mind, Major Dennis explained how to load and fire the Garand M-1 rifle: "Bolt forward, safety off, then squeeze the trigger." Charles went through the procedure several times to be certain that he understood.

Even as he practiced, he reached a decision. The battle was out in the open now. There would be no more of the skulking, dodging, and hiding of the underground war. He wanted to learn the new rules, to understand the war as he would be fighting it from now on. Charles knew that what he was doing was crazy, but the desperate struggle of the Airborne troopers had gotten into his blood. He had to do more than just round up lost soldiers. Armand and the others could handle that very well, but he—Charles—had a personal revenge to take on the enemy. Up ahead were the Nazis who had put Majo into that hellish camp.

Slinging a bandolier of ammunition over his shoulder, Charles grasped the rifle firmly and marched down to the road, following the paratroopers toward the fighting.

General Ridgway was standing in the open at a crossroads directing the men as they came up from the rendezvous. He grinned at the sight of Charles with a rifle in his hand, saluted approvingly, and pointed out the position the men were to take. *He's too good a target,* Charles thought, *with that bright yellow grenade shining in the sunlight. Still, that's what real leaders do.*

The sun was high now, and it was hot. The paratroopers moved through the dunes, pushing the stubborn enemy back from the approaches to the causeways, now and then pausing to allow the mortars to clear the ground before them. Run forward, drop, and fire. Duck when the mortar explodes close ahead, then rise and run forward again. Now and then, one of the paratroopers would stop suddenly, twist, and fall. There were calls for stretchers, cries of pain, yells of triumph, and whispered demands for more ammunition. And all the time, the enemy remained invisible to Charles. He wondered if the Americans around him could see any German soldiers.

From a shallow trench on top of a sand dune, Charles looked down on the beach and saw landing craft jolting up out of the water. Men bent under the weight of their packs poured out onto the sands on which dozens of motionless bodies reposed. There were little puffs all around them, but they ran forward, heads down, past their fallen comrades. The water was filled with what seemed like a thousand ships, and countless small boats were speeding toward the beach, circling between the white plumes of shell bursts. It was a fascinating sight, and Charles forgot why he was there until a soldier nudged him with the butt of his rifle and pointed to the ridge from which the enemy fire was coming.

Between the army advancing over the sands and the pressure from the paratroopers on the flank, it was soon over. By late afternoon, as the shadows lengthened, the Germans retreated and the seaborne landing continued without opposition. Exhausted, Charles sank back against the wall of his shallow firing pit and tried to make sense of what he had just seen and experienced.

It was not what he had thought war would be. No bugles, no flags waving, no sabers flashing, no clash of cavalry on an open plain—just death, bloody, anonymous death, just men being killed. All the books with their colorful pictures of Napoleon leading the massed ranks of bearded grenadiers against a redoubt, the cannons spouting flame, the smoke, the cheers . . . all the stories of military glory that he had heard as a boy, tales of Austerlitz and Jena and Wagram—suddenly all this had been reduced to a white-faced boy, with a thin trickle of blood at the corner of his mouth, strapped into a crushed glider. Dead in what was for him a foreign land. The few illusions Charles had had left after four years in the Resistance had vanished with the sight of that crumpled body. He had seen many men die this afternoon. The beach in front of him was still littered with motionless khaki-clad figures, but it was the picture of the dead glider pilot that haunted him. Charles could not understand why this should be.

War was the enemy. They fought the Germans because the Germans had made war. The Nazis must be destroyed so that war would be destroyed.

* * *

It was dark now, and by the light of lanterns the unloading was proceeding on the beach. All around Charles, slumped in their trenches, the paratroopers slept, still clutching their rifles. Tanks rumbled out of the sea and sputtered up onto the sand; landing craft swiftly discharged their cargoes and backed out. The first-aid men went from one motionless figure to another, giving what help they could. After the roar and confusion of the fight, it all seemed rather peaceful.

Charles walked down the dune toward the beach. He had suddenly realized that he was very hungry; perhaps someone would spare him one of the cans of field rations. As he made his way down the darkened beach, he heard someone speaking French nearby. Four men were standing near the bow of a landing craft, examining a map by the light of a flashlight. He could see that one of them wore the insignia of a colonel in the French army. He was a tall man with a trim mustache—clearly the man in command. He looked vaguely familiar even at that distance and in that light.

His heart pounding, Charles walked up to the group. Unnoticed in the darkness, he stood politely to one side while the colonel finished giving his orders for the debarkation. Then he coughed. As they turned, surprised at the interruption, Charles said, "Excuse me, Father, but what time do we eat in this damned army?"

They sat on the damp metal deck of the beached landing craft while Charles devoured the contents of two cans of army stew and washed it down with weak tea. "Delicious, is it not?" Colonel Marceau said with a wry smile. "Our allies may teach us a great deal about modern warfare, but they will never teach us anything about cooking." But to the famished Charles, the bland army stew really *was* delicious.

In the night surrounding them, they could hear the distant sounds of the fighting inland. Occasionally a salvo from one of the battleships would roar overhead like an aerial express train, and seconds later they would hear the explosions of the shells. On the beach, trucks rumbled, orders were shouted, and other landing craft splashed up onto the sands to unload.

Charles threw the empty cans over the side and leaned back against the bulkhead with a satisfied sigh. He politely refused the cigarette his father offered, which pleased the colonel. *He thinks I'm too young to smoke,* Charles thought, *and yet he knows I shot two men in Paris. That's not what a well-brought-up young man of nineteen is supposed to do.*

He had last seen his father in England almost two years before. The colonel had come on leave from his post in Algeria, and the family had been reunited at the seashore resort hotel where Charles' mother was living. The reunion had been warm, but Charles remembered that his parents had been made uneasy by the change in their son. Charles' father had expected to find the same loving, good-natured child he had left when he'd rejoined the army at the outbreak of the war. Instead, he had found a grown-up veteran of the Resistance still mourning his lost comrades. He had been proud, but he had sensed the new reserve in his son, and it had hurt him.

Now we meet as soldiers in the same battle, Charles thought, *and that pleases him. He never did care for the "cloak-and-dagger" role of a secret agent.*

"The invasion has changed the war," Colonel Marceau

said. "It is no longer an underground fight against an occupation army. Don't you think you should transfer to the Free French Army and help us clear France of the enemy? You have a lieutenant's commission, so it would be no problem."

"Transfer to Leclerc's armored division?" Charles' voice was noncommittal.

"As Leclerc's intelligence officer, may I point out that your knowledge of the present situation in France would be of great help in the battles ahead?"

"How soon does the division arrive?" Charles asked.

"As you know, that will depend on the progress in clearing the beaches, and how quickly we break out into open country. Perhaps two weeks or even three . . ."

Charles thought for a moment. "Thank you for the offer, Father, but I don't see myself sitting around waiting for General Leclerc. Besides, I have to wind up my mission, and right now I could be better employed helping our allies here in Normandy. They will need my knowledge of the situation. When the division arrives, we can talk about a transfer again."

His father looked at him questioningly. Charles smiled and gripped his hand reassuringly. "I know that you want me to serve in the regular army, Father, but I think you also want me to do my duty wherever my orders put me." He stood up and stared through the blackness down the crowded beach. "As you can see, the battle for Normandy isn't over yet. We're still sitting on the beaches."

6

Charles came out of the subway and walked across the sunlit square toward the taxi stand at the park entrance. A German patrol marched by, six heavily armed men led by a sergeant who threw a suspicious glance at the dark-haired young man with the shabby suitcase. Paris was a dangerous place for the Nazis in the third week of August, and the patrol was nervous. The police and the railroad workers were on strike, and, as the wounded from the Normandy front flooded into the city, rumors of an imminent uprising had everyone on edge.

He passed behind the patrol and stood on the street corner waiting. Every now and then he would look up and down the street as if expecting someone. But when a certain taxi moved to the head of the line, he threw his suitcase into the back of it, climbed in with a tired sigh, and said, "Bois de Boulogne, driver." The man at the wheel grunted, lit a cigarette, and shifted into gear.

The taxi pulled away from the curb, turned, and headed down the broad boulevard toward the Arc de Triomphe. When the driver was certain that they were not being followed, he turned again and drove through the entrance into the park. He was a heavyset man of about fifty, with graying hair and a small scar on his neck. Charles remembered when he had gotten that scar.

"Hello, Eagle," Charles said softly.

The driver did not take his eyes off the road. Switching the cigarette to the other side of his mouth, he answered over his shoulder. "Hello, Falcon. It's been a long time."

"Almost three years." They had not seen each other since the day the Vidal–Kléber network had been broken up and Charles had gone into hiding. One of his first acts had been to send a warning to Eagle, his second-in-command, that the group had been betrayed. According to plan, Eagle had dispersed their people until the danger was past.

"I recognized you at once," Eagle said. "You're taller now, not such a kid anymore. I remember that we had a hard time getting some of our friends to take you seriously, that's how young you looked. We heard that you had gotten to England, and there have been rumors that you were operating in Normandy just before the landings. Someone even said they had spotted you here in Paris last June. Is it true?"

Eagle drove slowly along the winding roads through the park. The Germans did not patrol this area; it would be too easy for someone to take a shot at them and then disappear among the trees.

"Yes. I saw Labru and tried to talk him out of sending his men into the streets to fight the Germans before the Allies arrived."

The driver grunted. "I bet you had no luck. It's going to happen any day now. All the arms they had stored in garages and apartments all over Paris have been distributed. A buddy of mine who's close to them showed me a copy of the orders that were sent out last night. As soon as the Allies get within eighty kilometers of Paris, the whole city will explode. They'll fight the Germans in the streets; they even plan to attack their headquarters at the Hôtel Meurice. It will be quite a battle."

"More like a massacre," Charles protested. "The Germans will level Paris before they allow the Resistance to take over—and they have all the heavy weapons. Labru is a fool."

The bitterness in his voice evidently shocked Eagle, who was silent for a moment. Throwing the cigarette butt out the window, he tried to explain the situation in Paris. "You've been away a long time, Falcon . . . three years. Every day for the last three years we have had to put up with the Boches. They've treated us like slaves, robbed us of everything that could be carted off to Germany, starved us—we've been cold, frightened, humiliated. They've shot hostages by the thousands, innocent people who got caught out after curfew or who tried to steal some coal or some food for their families. And we in the Resistance have been helpless to do anything about it. It has been fifty months since we lost the war—how many days is that?—and every hour, every minute has been a purgatory. They walk the streets like masters, pushing us off the pavements and parading their bands down the Champs-Elysées every morning to celebrate our defeat. Can you blame Labru for not wanting to let them crawl out of Paris without a fight?"

"But if there is no chance for victory? If it only means the destruction of the city?"

Eagle shrugged his shoulders. "France is more than a pile of stones called Paris. It has a soul and a spirit that does not reside only in buildings and bridges."

Charles found himself moved by the eloquence of this uneducated patriot. He thought of the countess, of Vidal and Kléber, of all those who had suffered for love of their country—and who still suffered. He remembered a slogan scrawled on a wall: "Paris remains French!" He had seen that slogan shortly after the Germans had entered the city in 1940. The young worker called Lynx who had painted those defiant words had later been the first Resistance worker to gun down a Nazi officer.

It was Lynx who had brought Charles into the Resistance. It was Lynx who had become his enemy because they had both loved the girl called Seagull, the girl Charles knew as Majo. Where was Lynx now? Leading one of Labru's action squads, getting ready to free Paris before the Allies did?

"No one wants to see Paris leveled, Falcon," Eagle continued, "but the sad truth is that the Resistance is divided into two groups. The Communists—Labru and his men—want an immediate uprising. They want to be masters of the capital before the Allies get here. Then, to rule Paris will be to rule France. The rest of us—those of us who take orders from de Gaulle—also want to kick out the Krauts, but we worry about what will happen to the city and its people. So we quarrel about it and the Communists go on getting ready while we do nothing. It's a mess."

"When will Labru strike?"

"Any day now, perhaps any hour. All he's waiting for is some indication that the Germans will leave Paris instead of defending it against the Allies. At the first sign of their departure, he will send his people into the streets."

"I must see him," Charles said desperately.

The driver shook his head. "Impossible, Falcon. He's

gone underground again. Only his closest comrades know where to find him. He won't appear again until the shooting starts."

Charles leaned back in the seat. His orders from General Leclerc, delivered to him by his father, had been very clear: proceed to Paris and evaluate the situation there; as soon as possible, report back. There was no mention of contacting Labru or of personally trying to prevent the uprising. Still, the situation was critical. Soon the first shot would ring out, a German soldier would fall, and the enemy would react with his usual fury. Paris would be destroyed.

Although his heart was pounding and he had a terrible headache, Charles forced himself to work it out logically. What would keep Labru from beginning the fighting? Orders from his superiors? Yes, but Charles had no control over that. A lightning dash to Paris by Leclerc's armored division? That had been ruled out by the Allies as too risky. In fact, the city was to be bypassed by the armies and taken much later. Suppose Labru and his staff were captured by the Gestapo? Charles shuddered even as the idea entered his head. *My God, I'm thinking of betraying a man who was my friend!* Silently Charles gave thanks that he did not know Labru's hiding place. It would be horrible to have to choose between Paris and Labru—especially since he knew in his heart that he would have to sacrifice Labru.

Charles caught Eagle watching him in the rearview mirror. *Can he guess how close I was to betrayal?* the younger man wondered.

If the Communists were planning to seize power, Charles thought, then there were certain key points they would have to take and hold: the Chamber of Deputies, which was the seat of political power; the City Hall; and, of course, the Prefecture of Police. Now, if one of those was held by a non-Communist Resistance group . . . "Eagle, how many people can you round up in the next twelve hours?"

Startled, the driver looked back over his shoulder at Falcon's tense face. "I don't know. Maybe fifty, sixty, or so. It depends on how many can be reached before curfew tonight, and how many are at home and not in hiding."

"Get the word out as quickly as possible. Tell them to bring whatever guns they have and to meet at seven tomorrow morning in the square in front of Notre Dame."

The driver grinned. "Are you planning to attack the cathedral, Falcon? What good would that do?"

"Not the cathedral, my friend. But just across the square—"

"The prefecture!"

"Yes. We're going to take and hold the prefecture against the Germans."

Exploding with laughter, Eagle pounded the wheel in glee. "Labru will split a gut. If we hold police headquarters, there is no way he can claim that the Communists liberated Paris . . . but can we do it?"

"Yes, I think we can. Taking the prefecture is no problem. With the police on strike, the place is almost deserted. Holding it is something else. But the Germans don't want to fight in Paris unless they are forced to. All they want to do is keep it open so that their troops retreating from Normandy can pass through in safety. The prefecture will be only a minor annoyance to them if it is not followed by a general uprising. They'll probe our position, of course, trying to find out how strong we are, but they'll be content to contain us so that we can't spread the revolt to the rest of the city."

"It's beautiful," Eagle said. "No one has ever captured

Paris without first taking the prefecture. But suppose Labru still orders a general uprising and grabs what power he can?"

Charles shook his head. "No, that wouldn't give him the prestige he needs to bring the Parisians over to his side. He'll have to wait and hope that the Boches drive us out of the prefecture, and then he'll make his move. . . . How many guns do your people have?"

"Not too many. We've been concerned with gathering intelligence, not with preparing for a fight. But don't worry, I know a garage in Montmartre where Labru's people have hidden arms. We'll just borrow some of those. Since Labru is so anxious to strike a blow for the liberation of Paris, he won't mind lending us the tools to do it with."

"Drop me back at the subway," Charles said. "You'd better get started rounding up your people. I'll see you tomorrow at seven in front of Notre Dame."

The only person who saw them was an elderly street sweeper, who almost dropped his broom in amazement. Charles led the *résistants* through the open gates, across the cobblestone courtyard, and into the gloomy gray building. With the police on strike, there was no one to stop them. A custodian who had been washing the front door took one look at their faces, threw his brush back in the bucket, and ran away.

In his apartment on the third floor, a sleepy prefect of police stared at the three armed men who marched into the room and told him that he was under arrest in the name of the French Republic and General de Gaulle. He barely had time to dress before he was hustled down to the basement and locked in a cell. It was Eagle who told him not to raise a fuss or they would have to shoot him.

Meekly, the prefect submitted to force. He knew that as a representative of France's pro-Nazi government he was hated by all Resistance workers.

There were thirty-seven men and women in the raiding party, but more would be coming. As soon as word of the capture of police headquarters spread, volunteers from all the different Resistance groups—everyone with the stomach for a fight—would rush to help defend the prefecture against the Germans. French patriots all over Paris would see this as their chance to strike a blow against the hated enemy and his Vichy minions. Charles expected many of the policemen now on strike to show up with their arms, and perhaps even some of Labru's people. . . . After all, even disciplined Communists sometimes remembered that they were French.

As he sent his people to their posts, ordered the barricading of the windows and doors, Charles worried anew about the Germans' reaction. He tried to imagine what would go on in the mind of the German commander of Paris, in his luxurious office in the Hôtel Meurice, when word was brought to him that "terrorists" had seized the prefecture. The first thing that would occur to General von Choltitz was that this was the initial step in a general uprising, and he would take immediate measures to protect the German garrison. After a while, it would become clear that the attack on police headquarters was an isolated incident, and that would puzzle the general. Being a military man and a typical methodical Boche, he would find it hard to understand what the Resistance hoped to accomplish by this reckless act. In any event, Charles was hoping that it would take him some time to figure it out and to take action against his little group.

Charles was inspecting one of the window barricades, a

jumble of desks and benches manned by two men with hunting rifles, when Eagle walked up to him with a broad grin on his face. "Look out there, Falcon," he said, pointing upward. "There's a sight we haven't seen for over four years."

Across the deserted courtyard, from a pole tied to the grille of a balcony, the red, white, and blue French flag hung triumphantly. Fearful of the patriotism it aroused, the Germans had forbidden its display all during the occupation. Now it floated defiantly over a small part of free France.

"It should make our people proud," Charles said casually. He knew that it would also inform the Germans that the prefecture had been taken.

The telephone rang loudly. "If it's for the prefect," Charles said, "tell them he's all tied up." Eagle laughed.

One of the men picked up the phone and muttered a few words. Then he said in surprise, "It's for you, Falcon."

"Hello?"

The voice on the other end was thick with anger. "What in the hell do you think you're doing?"

"Why, good morning, Labru. Haven't you heard? We've taken over police headquarters. We've got the prefect locked up in a cell, and we're waiting for the Germans to join the party. If you're not too busy, you might—"

"By whose orders have you occupied the prefecture?"

"General Leclerc's. He gets his orders from de Gaulle. Do you want to quarrel about it?" Charles' tone was light, but his heart was pounding. He suspected that Labru was virtually certain he was lying, and he could almost see the look of disbelief and fury on the ex-bartender's face. Charles was ready for the next question.

"Do you have these orders in writing, Falcon? I warn you that the Paris Resistance will not—"

"Falcon, look!" Eagle's urgent cry demanded Charles' attention. He put down the receiver and hurried to the window.

In the sunlit courtyard, a German staff car had stopped in front of the main entrance. As Charles and Eagle watched, the driver jumped out smartly and opened the door for his passenger, a captain of the General Staff. The officer returned his chauffeur's salute casually, then started up the steps. At the top, puzzled by the closed door and the absence of an usher to greet him, he stopped and peered about. It was clear that he was annoyed by the discourtesy being shown him. Then the chauffeur saw the French flag and shouted a warning.

Even as the captain stared unbelieving at the flag, the door behind him opened and he was seized and dragged sputtering inside. The driver started to run for the gate, but a well-aimed volley of rifle fire that splattered the ground ahead of him quickly changed his mind. He stopped, raised his arms in surrender, and marched up the steps to captivity.

"Put them with the prefect," Charles said. "No doubt the captain came especially to see him."

Eagle grinned and went off to give the orders.

Charles went back and picked up the receiver. "Hello, Labru. Did you hear that? Well, it doesn't matter now whether my orders are in writing or not. The Boches will be here soon, and they won't ask for credentials." He paused and listened to the heavy breathing for a moment. "Join the party if you wish. After all, most of our guns really belong to you. Don't wait for an invitation. We'll be too busy here to send them out."

He put the receiver back in its cradle. Inviting Labru to join the fight had been pure bravado, but they needed every fighter they could get. Besides, Charles knew he would not come.

Charles ordered the gasoline drained from the fuel tank of the German captain's staff car. This he had poured into empty wine bottles, which were then plugged with cotton rags. These Molotov cocktails would be their only protection against tanks and armored vehicles. Lighting the cotton and hurling the bottle against a tank would set the tank on fire, provided one could get close enough to hit the hot engine vents.

The defenders squatted behind the flimsy barricades and waited for the attack they knew would come.

All morning, men and women slipped into the building by twos and threes. Most of them were Eagle's people arriving late; some were Resistance workers from other groups. And some were just patriots who could not resist the opportunity to strike a blow against the enemy. One old man hobbled in clutching a 1918 rifle and proudly wearing the helmet he had worn at Verdun. A young woman brought in food and medical supplies and set up a first-aid station in the basement.

One of the last arrivals warned that a company of German infantry was massing across the square. Charles reinforced the guards at the main entrance and waited.

The attack came shortly after noon. Charles had just finished an inspection tour of the top floor, where he had stationed *résistants* with grenades and Molotov cocktails, when there was a warning shout from the main entrance. A burst of machine-gun fire shattered the lock on the gates and the Germans rushed into the courtyard, firing at the windows as they moved slowly toward the entrance.

There were about thirty, Charles estimated, led by a lieutenant. Battle-trained troops against his own amateurs.

Following orders, the defenders let the Germans reach the center of the courtyard. Then, from three sides, they poured a devastating hail of fire into the massed ranks of the enemy. Grenades from the top floor were hurled down to explode in the Germans' midst. The concentrated fire was too much for the attackers. The German lieutenant tried to rally what was left of his unit, but it was useless. The survivors wavered, then slowly withdrew, taking their dead and wounded with them.

Soon the courtyard was empty.

Two men ran out and gathered the weapons and ammunition. One waved a submachine gun triumphantly above his head. A cry of victory sounded from the prefecture as the defenders stood in the windows and cheered.

"We haven't won yet," Charles said to Eagle. "Find out what our losses are and report to me here."

Fifteen minutes later, Eagle was back with the report: three dead and seven wounded, two seriously. And the supply of ammunition was critically low—only about ten rounds per rifle remained.

It was quiet for the rest of the afternoon—ominously quiet. The enemy now knew that the prefecture was held in force. The next attack would be heavier: probably tanks and artillery. Charles inspected the walls and decided they would stand up to everything but shells of the heaviest caliber. As for tanks, the defenders would have to depend on the gasoline bombs; grenades would be useless. He wished he had two or three antitank mines to plant in the courtyard. Even better would be one of the rocket launchers that the Americans called "bazookas." During the fighting in Normandy, he had seen them used very effectively. But there was no point in dreaming about weapons he did not have; they would have to defend themselves with the few arms they had. *For how long?* Charles wondered. How many hours before they were overrun?

It was a long, nervous night. In the dark, more reinforcements crept in, but they were still few compared to the enemy. Charles visited the wounded in the basement hospital and spoke encouragingly to them, but he saw that they realized the peril of their position. The young nurse took him aside and whispered that one of the wounded would not live through the night. "Do what you can to make him comfortable," Charles said sadly. Even as they spoke, the man died.

At first light, there was some random sniper fire from an apartment house across a side street. It was inaccurate and only served to make the defenders keep their heads down. Some of the *résistants* wanted to shoot back, but Eagle ordered them to save their cartridges for a serious attack. It was demoralizing not to answer the annoying sniper fire, but, since it was doing no harm, it had to be tolerated.

A woman slipped in the side door with a basket of food and the rumor that a truce was being negotiated between the heads of the Paris Resistance and the German commander, General von Choltitz. It caused a lot of excitement in the besieged building. Perhaps the Allies were closer than they thought. Perhaps even now American tanks were entering Paris. Would the prefecture be relieved soon?

They were still speculating about when the Americans would appear when a German tank clanked into the square, rotated its turret slowly, and fired at the gate.

"So much for your truce!" Charles shouted. "Get ready with the Molotov cocktails!"

The tank smashed through the twisted remains of the iron grille gate and lumbered across the cobblestones of the courtyard, its cannon swiveling to cover the windows. A few futile shots ricocheted off its armor. "Hold your fire!" Charles ordered. "Wait until he's close enough!"

Waiting was too much to expect of men and women who were facing an advancing tank for the first time. A bottle sailed out of a top-floor window and smashed in flames in front of the tank. Then another, and another, all falling short but getting closer and closer. Charles cursed and sent Eagle up to take command.

But the shower of gasoline bombs burning on the cobblestones was too much for the tank crew. Its exhaust pipes spitting smoke, the tank backed out of range, still firing its cannon at the windows. Soon it disappeared through the gaping hole that had been the gate, turned, and clanked out of sight.

They had won the second battle. One man had been killed by the shelling.

They held the prefecture for three days against sporadic attacks. The Germans moved a field gun into position behind Notre Dame cathedral and started shelling, but the thick walls of the police headquarters did not crumble. Twice, small groups of German infantry penetrated into the courtyard, fired up at the windows, threw some grenades—but then quickly retired, carrying their wounded with them. They evidently had no desire to storm the citadel; rather, they seemed to want to test the resolve of the defenders, or perhaps to exhaust their ammunition. They left their dead sprawled in the courtyard, but took their weapons away.

Late on the afternoon of the fourth day, as Charles was inspecting the sentries, a German major appeared at the shattered gate followed by a soldier with a white flag.

"They want to parley," Eagle growled. "Shall I have them fired on?"

"No," Charles said. "I'll talk to him. At least it will gain us more time before the next attack, and perhaps I can learn something of what is happening in the city."

He ordered the desks barricading the front door removed and went out alone into the courtyard. Silently, the weary defenders stood at the windows and watched him stride boldly to the gate.

The German officer looked with disdain at the slim, dark-haired young man in shirt sleeves, a pistol stuck in his belt, who approached. "I'm Major Kessel, representing the German commander in Paris. I wish to speak to the officer commanding the terrorists in the prefecture."

"I'm Lieutenant Marceau, representing General Leclerc of the Free French Army now approaching Paris. I command the *soldiers* defending the prefecture. I'd advise you to lower your voice and speak more respectfully, major. Some of my soldiers might hear you and blow your head off to repay you for your arrogance."

The major stiffened and the color drained from his face. The soldier behind him tightened his grip on the staff of the white flag and stared, terrified, at the grim-looking men and women in the windows.

"I am under a flag of truce," the officer stuttered. *His French is not bad,* Charles thought, *except when he's nervous. I'd better act as if I have a thousand men behind me or he'll guess how weak we are.*

"That's the only reason you're standing here without a

hole in your hide. Now suppose you give me your message—and politely, or, white flag or no white flag, you're a dead man."

The German swallowed hard. From his tunic pocket, he took a folded sheet of paper, which he handed to Charles. He started to explain the contents. "A truce has been signed between—"

"I can read," Charles interrupted. It was the text of a cease-fire signed by the German commander and the heads of the Resistance. All German troops were to be confined to their barracks; no hostile acts were to be permitted on either side; the prefecture was to be evacuated, its defenders allowed to leave unharmed. As Charles had suspected, the enemy did not want war in the streets of Paris.

One thing worried Charles: among the names at the bottom of the truce paper, those of the Communist leaders were conspicuously missing. That meant that Labru could not be held to this cease-fire. If Charles and his men left the prefecture, Labru might send his people to occupy it, and then begin a general uprising in violation of the truce. But there was nothing he could do about that. . . .

"The cease-fire begins at midnight tonight," Charles said. Quivering with rage, the major nodded. He evidently did not trust himself to speak.

"Very well. Here is my signature to confirm that I have seen and will observe the terms of this document." Taking a pen from his shirt pocket, Charles wrote his name and rank across the bottom of the paper. He folded the sheet carefully and handed it back to the major.

"We would like permission to remove our dead from the courtyard," the major said stiffly.

Charles nodded. "Permission is granted. We will hold

our fire for thirty minutes. Make certain that any men you send are unarmed and that all vehicles are open. We don't want any surprise assaults from Red Cross ambulances at our front door. And major, just one more thing. Tell General von Choltitz that the next time he has a message for me he should use an emissary with better manners, or he will lose him permanently. . . . Thirty minutes, no more. We will fire a warning shot two minutes before the time is up."

Turning on his heel, Charles strode back across the yard and entered the building. As soon as he had passed through the door, the desks were quickly shoved back into place. Eagle looked at him inquiringly.

Charles tried to keep his voice matter-of-fact. "A truce has been signed. The cease-fire begins tonight at midnight. The Boches have pledged not to bother us while we leave."

"Do you trust them?"

"It's in their interest to observe the truce. Otherwise they would not have signed it. Can you imagine what it cost them to negotiate with 'terrorists'? No, they'll let us pull out. All they want right now is a peaceful Paris, nobody shooting at them while they get ready to run back to the fatherland."

"We'll be sitting ducks coming out into the square if the Boches break their word."

"That's why we're going out one by one over the back wall, starting at ten tonight. They expect us to hold here until the last minute—a matter of honor. But by midnight we'll be long gone."

Two days later, Charles walked down a quiet street not far from the Arc de Triomphe. An uneasy truce still lay over Paris, and people were staying close to home. Despite the cease-fire, Labru's men had erected barricades at many of the main intersections to show their strength. There had been skirmishes and fighting between Resistance workers and German soldiers. Everyone was waiting for the first sign of Leclerc's tanks, which were reportedly just thirty kilometers away.

Charles stopped in front of the familiar gray three-story building at number 93 rue Lauriston. It was deserted, its front door gaping open. Inside, the place was a shambles; Lafont's gang of French Gestapo agents had obviously left in a great hurry. Ripped furniture, overturned wardrobes, broken desks with their drawers scattered about the rooms; shutters hanging loosely at the windows; walls splashed with paint—Lafont's men had indulged in an orgy of destruction before fleeing to Germany. Papers, many of them with official stamps, were scattered everywhere.

He climbed the stairs to the second floor and entered what had been Lafont's office. Even in its present disarray, it made a cold shudder run through his body as he remembered the interrogation he had undergone here. At the window, he looked out onto the narrow balcony where he had hidden that awful night waiting for Pascal to be brought into the room. He fingered the latch of the iron shutter and remembered how he had lifted it from the outside with a knife blade. And this was where Pascal had been sitting. And the Gestapo captain had stood here.

For a moment, Charles' mind was immobilized by painful memories. Then he shook them off and got down to work.

The drawers of the two files had been pulled out and the contents scattered about the room. Paint had been splattered over the large mass of documents—red paint, the color of blood.

It took two hours of searching to find Majo's dossier. Luckily, it had been in a manila folder, and only the edges were stained red. Inside were two sheets of paper. On one was a short history of the arrest of the Vidal–Kléber network, the death sentences of nine men, and a report on further unsuccessful attempts to find the other members of the group. *Good old Eagle*, Charles thought. *He kept the others safe*.

The second page had only three entries:

> Marie-Josette Loubet, called "Seagull." Sentenced to twenty years imprisonment, December 9, 1941. Sent to Ravensbrück concentration camp. Prisoner #156478. Transferred to Kronau concentration camp after attempted escape, January 11, 1944.

The next day, August 25, the first squadron of Leclerc's tanks rolled into Paris. There were short, bitter fights as die-hard Nazis were shelled out of their strongholds. Then it was all over.

Paris—after fifty months of occupation—was free again.

In the midst of the excitement and turmoil at the War Ministry on the rue Saint-Dominique, Charles appeared and quietly reported back for duty with Leclerc's division. Then he went to the map room on the second floor and found a town called Kronau on a large-scale map of Germany.

7

The April rains had turned the field into a sea of mud. Boards had been put down in front of the operations tent, a large pyramidal affair set at the near edge of the woods just outside the German town. The only thing that distinguished this tent from the others was a tricolor pennant with a large gold numeral "two" on it hanging limply next to the entrance. All the tanks, half-tracks, weapons carriers, and other vehicles of Leclerc's Second Armored Division were dispersed in the surrounding fields under camouflage as a precaution against an air raid. *We haven't seen a German plane since last winter,* Charles thought as his jeep slithered through the mud toward the tent, *but it pays to be careful.*

Behind him, along the road that led to the small German town with the funny name, he could see the jeeps that the men of his reconnaissance squadron had covered with netting and branches. Next to them were the indistinct outlines of de Voisin's light tanks, their radio antennas sticking up through the camouflage. It was an impressive sight—the powerful armored striking force hiding under cover, waiting silently to move out for the next attack.

In the eight months since the liberation of Paris, the division had freed all of eastern France, fighting a hundred major and minor battles on the way. Among the hills and ravines of the Vosges mountains, they had taken the measure of the enemy, and always they had beaten him back. Their losses had been high; burnt-out tanks, shattered personnel carriers, and graves marked their victorious drive to clear France of the foe who had for so long stood on her soil.

In the fighting, Lieutenant Charles Marceau and Captain Henri de Voisin had distinguished themselves many times. Charles' jeeps had led the way, clearing the roads and searching out the enemy, and Henri's light tanks had followed closely to batter down any entrenched positions. They had left their dead on the hillsides and forest paths; the ravines were littered with the blackened shells of their vehicles. But the way had been cleared for the main thrust: the heavy tanks that had lumbered past the shattered remains of roadblocks and, last week, had gone across the Rhine into Germany. When the foe had attacked in the Ardennes last December and things had gone badly there, Leclerc had refused to withdraw to a safer line and had ordered a general assault to keep the Germans from sending in any reinforcements. It had been costly winter warfare, but it had helped contain the bulge in the Allied lines.

Now it was April, and soon the roads and fields would be dry. For five days, they had been sitting outside Weidenheim repairing the battle damage and refitting. Reinforcements had appeared. Today they were up to strength and eager to advance, for everywhere there were signs that the enemy was at his last gasp. Resistance was light and faint-hearted. Large groups of Nazis surrendered at the first shot. White sheets fluttered from the windows as Leclerc's division entered German towns, and more and more deserters were appearing in their lines, eager to buy their safety with information.

Inside the drafty operations tent, the acetylene lamps sputtered noisily and bathed everything in a yellow glow. There was a strong smell of leather and oil. To one side, a large situation map covered with green and red scrawls had been placed on an easel. The regimental and battalion commanders were seated expectantly on wooden benches, talking about past and future battles, and trying not to let their excitement show. It was clear that something momentous was in the wind. *Half of them,* Charles thought, *expect to get orders to drive through to Berlin. In this foul air, they can smell victory at last.*

He found a seat on a wooden bench next to de Voisin, who was wearing the mud-stained sheepskin jacket, whipcord breeches, and combat boots that were the standard dress for an officer in a French armored division on active service. Henri was old army; his family had served France as soldiers for four centuries, and he was a graduate of the military academy at Saint Cyr. Caught in Belgium by the defeat in 1940, he had fought his way to the port of Dunkirk and had been evacuated to England. He had refused to return to occupied France and had been one of the first evacuees to join de Gaulle and the Free French. He had earned his captaincy at twenty-six in the fighting in North Africa, and the Military Medal for valor in Normandy. Bold, adventurous, and peppery, he was admired by his fellow officers and adored by his men. He and Charles shared a love of action that had earned them the title of "the front-line twins."

"Hello, Henri. What's this all about?" Charles pointed to the map.

De Voisin shrugged his shoulders eloquently. "Who knows, Charles? Perhaps we are going to drive on to Berlin and put Hitler in a cage. On the other hand, we may be in for a lecture on the danger of mixing with the *Fräuleins*. I understand we are losing more men to venereal disease than to bullets."

"I wouldn't be a bit surprised," Charles said. "I've had a hard time keeping my men from taking girls out for joyrides. Still, after what they've been through these last six months, who can blame the poor devils?"

De Voisin jerked his head toward the entrance. "We'll soon know what's up. Here comes the bad news."

They stood at attention as Colonel Marceau entered the tent, followed by his adjutant. Standing in front of the map, he motioned them back to their seats.

"Gentlemen," he began, "the division commander is attending a meeting of senior officers. I spoke to him on the telephone about an hour ago, and he asked me to inform you of one of the decisions that has been reached."

The colonel paused and looked the audience over. There was absolute silence.

"We have been informed that advance elements of the Soviet army are rapidly approaching Munich from the east. As you know, the Russians are presently fighting in Berlin, and it is possible that we will meet them any day now. In order to avoid any unfortunate incident in which we might fire on each other, the high command has decided that we are to hold our position here until the location of our Soviet allies is firmly established."

There was a murmur of stunned disbelief. Charles started to rise to protest. Henri grabbed his sleeve and pulled him back into his seat. A man in the back of the tent gave voice to the general anger. "The Germans occupied France for over four years, killed, looted, and humiliated us—and we are to sit here doing nothing?"

The colonel stared grimly around the tent. "Those are our orders, and you gentlemen will be expected to obey them."

A major stood up. "What shall I say to the families of the men we lost getting here, colonel? Shall I tell them that we got tired of fighting for France? Shall I say that their son, their brother, their husband, or their father died uselessly because we are going to let the Boches sit peacefully in their trenches a mile away?"

"Tell them that no German now stands on French soil," the colonel said proudly. "Then tell them that we are soldiers and that we obey orders. And that, gentlemen, is all you can say. Dismissed."

Sick at heart, Charles sat gloomily while the other officers filed slowly from the tent. The orders had come as a stunning blow to him. For months now, he had been fuming impatiently as the division slowly carried the battle into Germany. There was a map in his tent on which daily he had marked the miles gained toward a spot just west of Munich that was the Kronau concentration camp. It had come closer and closer, until it seemed that one violent dash would bring him to his goal, and then he would free Majo from hell itself. And now this . . . to stop here, while their fellow countrymen and countrywomen were still rotting in those hellholes—that was unthinkable.

I'll never make a good army officer, Charles thought grimly. *I can never believe that orders from a superior are the only law a man should follow. After all, I had no orders to take the Paris prefecture. . . .*

Majo, hold on. I'm coming.

He felt Henri's hand on his shoulder. He looked up and caught his friend's sympathetic gaze.

One night, after a long, bitter fight out of an ambush, Charles and Henri had sacked out side by side under a truck. They had been too excited to sleep, and had talked for hours. Charles had gone on and on about the Resistance, about Vidal and Kléber, his own escape from the Gestapo . . . and about Majo, the lovely Seagull, and what she meant to him. And Henri had seen the map, had watched silently more than once as Charles marked their progress toward Kronau. So Henri knew.

Smiling wanly, Charles murmured, "I'm all right now." He got up slowly from the bench.

Colonel Marceau had made it clear that he, too, knew about Majo; Charles' mother must have told him. *I must not lose my damned temper,* Charles thought. He took a deep breath and walked to the front of the tent.

Colonel Marceau was standing at the map talking to his adjutant, and Charles waited respectfully for him to finish. The orders were brief. The adjutant saluted and left the tent, followed by an anxious de Voisin.

"Colonel?" His father turned. "I assume that reconnaissance will still be allowed—to determine if the enemy is about to make a move."

The colonel nodded, but there was a forbidding look on his face. "Your jeeps and some of de Voisin's light tanks will patrol our front daily, but no more than three kilometers from this position. You will start at dawn and be back no later than noon. Another patrol will take over then." He drew a heavy red line on the map. "Do I make myself quite clear, lieutenant? Three kilometers in front of our present position *and no farther!*"

He obviously knew what Charles had in mind. Charles felt the anger welling up in his chest and fought it down. When he spoke, his voice was edgy but formal.

"Sir, I request permission for individual action at my own discretion in case the enemy—"

"Refused! Your orders are clear."

"May I respectfully ask permission to see the divisional commander?"

"For what purpose?"

"A private matter, sir."

"General Leclerc is busy coordinating plans with the Americans. He cannot be bothered with the private affairs of junior officers at this time. Request refused."

Charles swallowed hard and stared angrily at his father. "Colonel, I would like an immediate transfer to the American armored division on our left. As a liaison officer, I could—"

"A transfer is out of the question," the colonel interrupted. For the first time, his face and voice softened. "Your superior tells me that you are a first-rate officer, invaluable to the command, a good leader, and a fighter. No more than I would expect, of course." He gripped Charles' shoulder affectionately. "I know what you are thinking, my boy, but it is reckless and suicidal. You are an officer now, and responsible for the lives of your men. I know what this girl means to you, and your feelings do you honor, but you have a duty to your squadron."

"A duty to sit here on my rump doing nothing in the face of the enemy?"

His father stiffened and jerked his hand from his shoulder. Charles' sarcasm was dangerously close to insubordination. "A duty to obey orders and not to imperil your men for a private matter."

"Colonel, I beg you—"

"No, an officer does not beg. You have your orders, lieutenant. Obey them. You are dismissed."

Charles saluted, turned on his heel, and marched from the tent.

Henri de Voisin looked up inquiringly as Charles stormed into the tent they shared, but he refrained from asking about the conversation after one glance at his friend's furious face. Charles threw his jacket onto his cot, took his secret map from his footlocker, and stood in the corner studying it. He found a ruler, checked a distance, and sighed as he arrived at the answer.

After ten minutes, de Voisin broke the deep silence. "I think you'd better take me with you, old man."

Startled, Charles looked up at his friend. "Take you where?"

Henri walked over and pointed to a dot on the map. "There," he said quietly. The dot was a little town just west of Munich: Kronau.

"Henri, it is one hundred twenty-eight kilometers from here. You know the odds against our getting there."

De Voisin studied the road network. "Well, it won't be easy, no vacation trip," he said, "but if we can reach the *Autobahn*, this new highway here—" he stabbed at the map—"we should have a chance. Say thirty-two kilometers an hour for my tanks; that makes it about four hours, depending on what opposition we hit. If we start at midnight, we'll be there just before first light. We'll have a better chance in the dark."

"But you're a career officer, Henri. If I get court-martialed for disobeying orders, well, so what? But you'll be cashiered for this."

His friend shrugged his shoulders. "You'll never make it alone. Your jeeps are too vulnerable, and you've only got a couple of machine guns for firepower. No, you need my tanks to get through. So I'm inviting myself along. As for my career—well, it is *my* career, and if I want to risk it—"

"Henri, I—" The words of gratitude stuck in Charles' throat. He could only grasp his friend's hand and squeeze it.

"A raid behind enemy lines," Henri said with a grin. "Now, that's more like the war we read about as children. Much better than all this slogging and punching we've done up to now. When do we go?"

"We'll do our routine patrol tomorrow morning and find a hole in the enemy lines where we can get through." Charles spoke with mounting excitement. "Back at noon as ordered, refuel, then out again after midnight. We'll park the tanks and jeeps far enough from headquarters so they won't hear us leave."

They shook hands again, solemnly. Then Henri said, "I suppose the colonel said something to you about risking your men's lives. Well, I suggest we tell the men about all those poor devils in that living hell called Kronau and ask for volunteers. By now, they're so angry about this halt that we'll have more than we can take along."

It happened exactly as de Voisin had predicted. That night, after mess, Charles explained the mission to his men. He talked about the risks and then told them what they might expect to find in a German concentration camp. Before he could finish and call for volunteers, they all pressed forward, eager to go. In the end, he had to appeal to their love of gambling: he had them put their dog tags in a helmet and then drew out eleven names. With himself, enough to man three jeeps.

The next day, the reconnaissance patrol left at the crack of dawn. When it returned at noon, the route around the enemy lines was carefully sketched on Charles' map.

The moon rose shortly after midnight, bathing the fields in a soft silver light, and soon three jeeps and two tanks slipped out of the fields onto the road. The sentries were puzzled, because they had not been informed of the mission, but they did not challenge the convoy. Night reconnaissance was not uncommon, and they assumed that "the front-line twins" were acting on orders as usual. Charles returned their salute casually, as if he were off on a routine assignment.

The vehicles passed through Weidenheim, the rumbling of their engines echoing from the dark, silent houses. Charles knew that behind those blacked-out windows, German civilians were listening fearfully, wondering if war was coming back to them. The limp white sheets, signs of the enemy's will to surrender, hung like ghostly banners from many of the neat housefronts.

They passed the stone church at the far edge of the town and drove steadily into the open countryside, past dark fields of hops and barley, farmhouses and barns, and, once, a shattered factory, its roof open to the sky. It was an eerie sight. It could have been a Goya sketch of the devastations of war in black and silver. Charles felt a chill that had nothing to do with the night air.

Ten minutes later, they reached the crossroads that marked the Allies' farthest advance. Less than two hundred yards ahead, strung out along a railroad embankment, small groups of German soldiers were dug in, waiting for the first sign of a French attack. They were in radio communication with their artillery, and, at the first alert, shellfire would exact a fearful toll from the attackers. At the crossroads, the convoy turned left and took the road that led into the woods, paralleling the German positions. From the main road, a narrow dirt path, just wide enough for the tanks, led off to the right. They had scouted the route that morning, testing the path to make certain that it could bear the weight of a light tank. It was wet and muddy, but firm underneath.

The moonlight helped enormously. They could see the obstacles on the road and could proceed without headlights, avoiding the risk of detection. Once, they stopped to remove a fallen tree that blocked the path. They worked silently, for in the deathly quiet of the woods even a soft curse would carry far.

The path twisted and turned, crossed a ravine, and then led down to the stream marked on Charles' map. The water was only axle deep. They drove across, up a steep slope, and onto a tarred road in open country.

Picking up speed, they rolled down the empty road. The only sound was from the motors and from the metallic clatter of tank treads on the hard surface. Alert for the first sign of the enemy, Charles peered anxiously into the darkness ahead. A truck convoy running without headlights—or, worse, an enemy armored column—could be upon them before they could hear or spot it.

The corporal driving Charles' jeep was chewing nervously on an unlit cigar. Charles found that his palms were wet with perspiration, but decided not to do anything so obvious as wiping them. Instead, he thrust them into the pockets of his jacket, leaned back nonchalantly, and tried to appear unconcerned. The corporal grinned, but Charles suspected that he was not fooled by the gesture.

A little after one-thirty the dark outlines of a cluster of houses appeared. Charles drew a circle around the name ULM on his map and wrote in the time. He motioned the driver to turn left on a side road that would skirt the town; then he turned to make certain that the rest of the convoy followed them. They were behind the German lines now, and Charles was surprised that no troops were guarding the approaches to Ulm. Was the enemy more demoralized than they had estimated? Were the Germans in full retreat, leaving only small, desperate units behind as a rear guard?

They drove up a hill. Glancing back, Charles saw the whole town brooding ominously in the valley below. Not a light showed. Were they asleep, Charles wondered, or hiding behind those dark windows, waiting for the enemy?

The road crossed a short, narrow bridge, then swung around to parallel the Danube River and a railroad track. Checking his map, Charles noted that the *Autobahn* was less than five miles ahead. Another ten minutes should see them there.

Suddenly, he heard a high-pitched whistle. As he looked around frantically, the driver pounded his shoulder and pointed down the track ahead of them.

A train came around the bend and chugged slowly in their direction. Only the dark outline could be seen, lighted now and then by a flare of sparks from the smokestack. As it passed not fifty yards away, they saw a long line of freight cars, then a section of flatbeds with the bulky outlines of tanks tied to them. The Germans were moving reinforcements up to meet Leclerc's division!

Charles hesitated for only a moment. If he revealed his presence behind the lines, they might never get to Kronau, but the threat to the Allied forces was too great to ignore.

He ordered the jeep driver to stop and ran back to the lead tank. Henri leaned down from the turret. "The train, Henri!" Charles yelled.

With a broad grin, de Voisin picked up a microphone and quickly gave a command. The turrets of the two tanks revolved with agonizing slowness until they pointed at their target.

"Fire!"

At point-blank range, the two cannons fired. With a shrill scream of escaping steam, the locomotive exploded and rolled off the track, carrying the first three freight cars with it. Behind him, Charles heard the rattle of the machine guns on the jeeps as his men raked the train.

The ambush lasted only three minutes, but it seemed like hours. Henri's tanks worked their way down the line of cars, smashing them like toys. One freight car filled with ammunition exploded in a blaze of light, setting fire to the flatbeds holding the tanks. Soon the whole train was ablaze from end to end, and the pitifully small band of survivors had taken refuge in the ditches and was starting to shoot back.

Charles ran back to his jeep and signaled the column forward. As they moved off down the road, the two tanks continued to pump shells into the blazing wreckage, forcing the defenders to keep their heads down. There were two more explosions, then a huge fiery cloud as a tank car full of oil blew up.

It was over. The threat to Leclerc's division from this armored column was gone. Charles settled back in his seat, watching the road ahead. He had done his duty, but now the Germans knew that a small raiding party of tanks and jeeps was behind their lines. They also knew where it had been at a given time, and the direction in which it had gone.

At the *Autobahn*, a squad of motorcyclists stared in astonishment as the jeeps and tanks roared out of the night. A brief burst from the machine gun in the first jeep and they disappeared hastily, leaving the road open. It worried Charles that they had not put up more of a fight. In any case, they would be waiting with bigger guns when the little convoy came back.

The broad concrete road ran straight as an arrow down toward Munich. Charles spotted a truck or two in the distance, and once a dispatch rider hurried past with a wave of the hand. In the dark, it was hard to tell friend from foe. They let him pass unharmed.

Two hours later, the convoy turned off onto a hardtop road with a sign pointing to Kronau.

The horizon was just beginning to lighten with streamers of red and orange when they spotted the barbed wire fences of the camp.

8

As the sun rose, they could see the camp more clearly: forty or fifty wooden barracks, a few one-story brick buildings clustered near the main gate, a power house, a large metal structure with a curved roof—all set in a muddy plain and surrounded by a double line of barbed wire. From a flagpole, the crooked black spider of the swastika fluttered on a blood red background. High watchtowers were spaced along the perimeter of the camp, and, through their field glasses, Charles and Henri saw that they were empty.

There was no one at the half-opened gate, no one in the streets between the barracks—no guards, no inmates, no one.

Kronau was deserted.

They drove down slowly, fearful of a trap. Above the gate, a sign proclaimed ARBEIT MACHT FREIHEIT—"Work Is Freedom." Everywhere there was the same deep, brooding silence. Henri left one tank at the entrance to cover them as they rolled up to the first brick building, marked COMMANDANT'S OFFICE. Charles got out of his jeep and stood anxiously looking around. The quiet was nerve-wracking. Where was everyone?

"Corporal Lebrun, take six men and search the barracks," he ordered. "Faillot, take the other three and drive around the perimeter. See what you can find." Charles walked over to Henri's tank. "We'll search the camp. Better have someone manning this tank just in case we need help. If we get into trouble, we'll fire two shots."

"Keep your eyes open, Charles," Henri warned. "There may be some die-hard S.S. men lurking in one of those buildings. I'll take a look in there—" he jerked his chin toward the commandant's office—"and see if I can find out what happened here. This place makes my flesh crawl."

Charles nodded and walked off down a muddy street, pistol in hand, alert for any sign of trouble. Everywhere there were indications of a hasty withdrawal: papers, articles of clothing, a few pots and pans scattered about. The door of one building was half torn off, as if the occupants had rushed out, fleeing in terror. Charles peered inside one of the unpainted barracks and was assailed by the sour smell of unwashed flesh. There were about fifty wooden plank beds in tiers of three, a small cast-iron stove—cold—and piles of garbage and debris. A crude hand-lettered calendar was nailed next to the door; the date it showed was April 22—yesterday.

The bitterness of his failure overwhelmed him. He had failed in his mission by twenty-four hours. Sometime yesterday, the S.S. guards had routed the inmates out of these stinking barracks and had driven them down the road deeper into Germany. Somewhere out there, the long column of feeble men and women was being whipped along by S.S. troops fearful of the advancing Allies.

But where? In which direction had they gone, and how far ahead were they?

As Charles stood wearily in the door of the barracks trying to deal with the emptiness of his defeat, de Voisin came around the corner. He reached into the pocket of his tunic and drew out a crumpled card. Thrusting it into Charles' hand, he said quickly, "I found it in the files in the commandant's office. I guess they didn't have time to burn them all. I thought you would want to know." He turned on his heel and hurried away.

Charles turned the card over slowly, reluctant to read it. For some strange reason, he knew what it said. Perhaps he had known all along and had only come here to be certain that it was so.

> LOUBET, MARIE-JOSETTE, #156478.
> Entered January 11, 1944.
> Died of typhus, March 6, 1945.

There were a few other details: her work assignment (the kitchen), her room assignment (barracks 27, bed 15), and the ominous symbol N–N. *Nacht und Nebel.* Night and fog, Charles translated. A code phrase. In other words, never to leave alive, but to disappear finally, without a trace.

A death sentence for Majo. The Seagull was to vanish.

Sentence carried out.

Wearily, Charles dropped the card on the ground and walked away. It was over. All these years of waiting, wanting, dreaming—all finished by a single scrawled line in German on a dirty card.

Majo was dead.

His mind blank from the pain that had driven out even grief and remorse, he stumbled among the buildings. The numbers were written in red paint next to the doorways, and unwillingly he found himself outside barracks 27. Why should he want to see it? What good would it do now? Majo wasn't there. She wasn't anywhere.

Bed 15 was no different from the others, a bare plank at the bottom of a tier of three. He tried to picture her there, shivering under a thin blanket, roused at dawn by the cries of the female trusties, beaten with a truncheon if she was too slow . . . but the image of Majo imprisoned refused to appear. Instead he saw her stretched out on the bed of hay that night they'd come back from Vichy. He smelled the warmth of her body and felt her arms about his neck.

He ran his hand over the rough wooden post above the bed. Outside, someone was calling his name, but he did not move.

Then he saw the message.

She had cut it slowly and painfully into the post, probably using the edge of a spoon. It was not very deep; her strength must have been failing, and perhaps she had known that she was dying. It was there. Her last words. No appeal to patriotism, no last defiant proclamation, nothing about the Resistance and France—just four words, a cry from a dying girl to a boy she had not seen in over three years.

FALCON GIVE ME COURAGE

"Majo," Charles whispered. "You did not forget, and I never will. I loved you then, I love you now, and I always will. Good-bye, Seagull, my comrade, my only love."

He walked out of the barracks and down the street to the commandant's office. Henri and the others were waiting for him there. No one said a word. One look at his face was enough.

Charles climbed into his jeep. "Let's go," he said. "We're finished here."

The tank blocking the entrance moved off to allow the jeeps to pass. The little convoy drove through the gate, climbed the hill, and started back toward the *Autobahn.*

Charles did not look back.

"It is a miracle," General Leclerc said, "that you were not wiped out. One hundred thirty kilometers . . . and then back by the same route. Just one antitank gun blocking the road, and—" He shook his head in wonder at such insanity.

The informal court of inquiry was held an hour after their return to camp. Charles and Henri had dismissed the men with praise and thanks, and then had reported themselves under arrest to the general. Confined to their tent, they had written a brief report on the trip, mentioning the episode of the train and stating that they had not encountered any strong resistance behind the enemy lines. They told what they had found at Kronau, and how on the return trip all the towns they had passed through had been eager to surrender.

It was a military report, so nothing was said of Majo.

Colonel Marceau leaned over and whispered into the general's ear. Leclerc nodded, then cut him off with a wave of the hand. The other member of the court, the colonel commanding the division artillery, stared bemusedly at the two young men standing at a rigid attention in front of the flag-draped table. It was clear that he did not know what to make of such flagrant disobedience of orders.

"From your report, I take it that you met no Russians out there?" Leclerc's question was addressed to Henri, as the senior officer.

"No, sir. No sign of any troops other than German—and few of those. There seems to be nothing in front of us but the lightest screen of motorcyclists and small rearguard units. Except for the train, we saw no signs of any active attempt at resistance in this sector."

The general grunted thoughtfully. "I've sent that information on to corps headquarters. No doubt they will draw the logical conclusion about this mad trip of yours. While I admit that this reconnaissance has been invaluable, it does not excuse your violation of clear orders to go no farther than three kilometers beyond our present position. Have you any excuse to offer?"

Charles remembered the army tradition that "an officer never offers excuses. If he violates a regulation, he accepts the punishment without trying to soften it by explaining." The two young men remained silent, their eyes fixed on a point above the general's head.

"Very good," Leclerc said approvingly. "At least now you act like officers in the French army." He glanced at the two colonels as if seeking advice, but they refused to meet his eyes. This was a matter for the commanding general alone to decide. Colonel Marceau started to say something, then stopped. He looked at his son and shook his head sadly.

Sorry, Father, Charles thought miserably, *but I had to do this.*

"Ordinarily," the general said, "such a gross violation of orders in the face of the enemy would call for a full court-martial, which would undoubtedly exact the severest of penalties. You both deserve to be broken in rank and dismissed from the army." He paused and looked thoughtfully at the report on the table in front of him. "I see only one mitigating factor—the valuable information that this disgraceful episode revealed. I will not hide from you that my superiors are very pleased with what they call 'our gallant initiative in reconnaissance.' Of course, they don't know the whole story, and I have no intention of informing them of the lack of discipline that two of my officers have shown. Let them think we are a bunch of tigers."

He stood up and put on his kepi. The two colonels followed suit. Sentence was now to be pronounced.

"Captain de Voisin and Lieutenant Marceau are confined to quarters while off duty for one month. All leave and privileges are revoked for three months. One-half their pay is to be withheld for six months. Dismissed."

Charles and Henri saluted, turned, and marched from the tent. Outside, they stared at each other in amazement. They had gotten off unbelievably lightly. The general would let higher headquarters believe that he had ordered this reconnaissance mission rather than break two promising young officers—or perhaps, as a Frenchman, he had understood what had motivated them: love and friendship.

Later that day, Charles was summoned to Colonel Marceau's tent. As he entered, he was surprised to see Louise seated at a table, arranging papers in a file. She did not look up.

"We are preparing a fuller report for corps headquarters," his father said, "and there are a few details missing. Perhaps you can supply them. You may stand at ease."

Charles relaxed and looked questioningly at Louise. The colonel did not enlighten him, but simply nodded to her that he was ready to begin. Louise picked up a pad of paper and a pencil with which to record the conversation.

"Did you note any identification," the colonel asked, "or any unit markings on the tanks on the train you shot up?"

Charles shook his head. "No, sir. They were all under

canvas. There were also some half-tracks, but it was too dark to spot any markings."

"But you are certain they were all destroyed—or at least put out of action for a long time?"

"Absolutely certain. What our shelling did not demolish, the fire finished off. As we drove away, we heard the ammunition inside the tanks blow up from the heat."

"You mentioned running into some roadblocks. What sort of troops were they?"

"Twice it was motorcycle reconnaissance units armed only with light weapons. Once I thought it was some old men of a Home Guard platoon, but they ran away so quickly I couldn't tell."

"This bridge near Ulm. Will it take heavy tanks?" The colonel indicated the position on a map.

"No, sir, I don't think so. It's masonry, but light and narrow. I don't think it would take the weight. But there is a railroad bridge down here that probably could."

The colonel studied his papers. "Your report on the Kronau concentration camp is quite detailed. We've suspected for a long time that it was a death camp, but this is the first proof we've had. Frightful business . . ."

He looked up at his son, a question in his eyes. Charles returned the look impassively. No, he could not share the pain even with his father. Nor with Louise.

The next question came like a blow. "Did you find any proof that a French citizen had been confined to that camp?"

There was a long silence. Neither the colonel nor Louise looked at Charles as he groped for an answer.

"Among the scattered files in the office of the camp commandant, we found a card on a Frenchwoman who had been an inmate."

"Name?"

"Marie-Josette Loubet."

"Age?"

"Twenty-two."

"Address?"

"Twenty-seven rue Florian, Paris."

"Why was she in Kronau?"

"She was a member of a Resistance network in Paris that was broken up in November, 1941. Nine men were shot. Majo, I mean Mademoiselle Loubet, and another woman were sent first to Ravensbrück concentration camp."

"So we can assume that this young woman and other French citizens were moved deeper into Germany just before you arrived."

Wearily, Charles shook his head. "Mademoiselle Loubet died of typhus in March. It was on the card." *Now they know.*

The colonel half rose from his chair. "Oh, Charles, I—" But the look on his son's face allowed no expressions of sympathy. He slumped back and closed the file in front of him. "Thank you, lieutenant, that is all. Lieutenant Kellerman, have those notes typed up and sent to the general for review and transmission to corps."

Charles saluted and marched out without a glance at Louise.

That evening at mess, Charles' fellow officers were full of congratulations for "the front-line twins." Charles and Henri were heroes to the younger men and a source of amazement to the older ones. Their intrepid dash through the enemy lines was an inspiring and heroic episode, made even more thrilling by the rumors of their attempted rescue of the inmates of a concentration camp. In the midst of a war that had been mostly brutal slugging, it was a story to be repeated over and over again.

A tank captain came up to Charles and without a word solemnly shook his hand. Drinks were thrust upon him, and when he refused, no one was offended. They simply drank his health again and again. *They think me a hell of a fellow,* Charles thought bitterly, *ready for any wild action. And all I did was endanger a dozen men in a reckless search for a dead girl.*

The constant attention was too much for him. He toyed with his meal, then fled the mess tent, leaving Henri to enjoy the adulation. In the darkness, he wandered down to the motor pool to inspect the jeeps. That at least was his duty, and he wanted to be alone.

He exchanged a few words with the sentries, then walked slowly down the long line of vehicles. When he came to his jeep, he climbed into the front seat and sat quietly, brooding.

His thoughts were confused, but he knew that he had come to the end of something terribly important. Majo's death had put a period to all the events of the past four and a half years. The war was almost over and he had no idea of what to do with his life. At sixteen, he had joined the Resistance; there had been no time then to think of what sort of career he might have after the war. No one had talked about the end of the struggle—it had seemed so far away then, and, besides, it would have been dangerous to dwell on it. Dreaming of the future would have taken away from the constant alertness that had kept the *résistants* alive.

When he had lost his friends, his only friends at that time, his one thought had been revenge—and to find Majo again one day. Well, they were all dead now—Vidal,

Kléber, Majo—all gone. And they had left him alone, alive, and in his self-pity he almost regretted it. Better to have fallen at the execution stake with the others than to face the future alone. What would he do with himself? The game was over. The "great game" was finished.

The army? His father would like that, but Charles did not think that the peacetime army would suit him. Besides, his defiance of orders clearly showed that he did not have the temperament to be a regular army officer. No, the Marceau military tradition would end with his father . . . and his own record in this war. At least the family need not be ashamed of what he had done.

The thought of going back to Paris and trying to pick up the pieces of his former life frightened him. After all he had been through, all he had seen, how could he sit in a classroom and listen to some dull professor talk of literature or history? How could he walk down those streets, with all their sad memories?

No, he would leave France with its ghosts and go to America. He had not seen his mother's country since he was a child, but he remembered his grandfather, his strength and his kindness. His grandfather would help him find himself.

Sitting quietly in the jeep, surrounded by the familiar smells of oil, leather, and gasoline, he felt the tensions slip away. True, he had lost people he loved, but so had hundreds of thousands of others in five years of war. As a soldier's son, he could only consider his service as an honor and a privilege. And he had been good at it—Falcon and Lieutenant Marceau would both be remembered. Yes, he could be proud of what he had accomplished.

He had lost, but he had also won. The Lieutenant Charles Marceau of Leclerc's Second Armored Division was a man—tough, confident, able—not a boy any longer. *And I should not be sitting here moping,* Charles thought. He took a deep breath of the cool, pine-scented air. There! That was better!

Above the eastern horizon, a thin red and orange flame rose slowly into the night sky, then disappeared into some high clouds. *A German V-2 rocket,* Charles thought. *The enemy's dying gasp.*

Louise came out of the darkness, climbed into the jeep, and sat next to him. Charles acknowledged her presence with a smile, and they sat for a while without saying a word. Then she leaned over and took his hand tenderly, as though she knew he needed comforting. He did not pull it away.

It was a vow, the testimony of a woman who loved him. *Somewhere, somehow,* Charles thought, *I must make room in my life for Louise.* Majo would understand that he didn't want to be alone.

He squeezed her hand gently to let her know that he understood what she was offering.

About the Author

MILTON DANK was born and raised in Philadelphia. He received his B.A. and Ph.D. in physics from the University of Pennsylvania after serving in France as a combat glider pilot with the First Allied Airborne Army in 1944–45. As squadron translator and liaison officer with the French civil authorities after the liberation of France, he became interested in the story of the French under the Nazi occupation. He has written a nonfiction work on this period, *The French Against the French,* and a narrative history of the glider war, *The Glider Gang;* he is also the author of *The Dangerous Game,* a novel that tells of Charles Marceau's adventures as a French Resistance agent early in World War II. Dr. Dank lives with his wife and two daughters in Wyncote, Pennsylvania.